Jewel cases

Five Classic Mysteries of Theft

JOURNEY FORTH™

Greenville, South Carolina

Library of Congress Cataloging-in-Publication Data

Jewel cases : five classic mysteries of theft.
   v. cm.
  Contents: The Lenton Croft mystery / by Arthur Morrison—The
Azteck opal / by Rodrigues Ottolengui—The adventure of the blue carbuncle / by Sir Arthur Conan Doyle—The episode of the diamond
links / by Grant Allen.
   ISBN 1-57924-841-1 (alk. paper)
   1. Detective and mystery stories. [1. Mystery and detective stories.
2. Short Stories.]
   PZ5.J55 2002
   [Fic]—dc21

                        2002003593

Jewel Cases: Five Classic Mysteries of Theft
Designed by Erin Elizabeth Byram

©2002 Bob Jones University Press
Greenville, SC 29614

ISBN 1-57924-841-1

15 14 13 12 11 10 9 8 7 6 5 4 3 2 1

Publisher's Note

The stories of Victorian mystery writers often made their first appearance in the periodicals of the day. In many cases these same stories were collected into a book and were published a few months or years later. Happily for the mystery buff there was no shortage of detective stories.

Sir Arthur Conan Doyle created the quintessential detective of the genre, the observant Sherlock Holmes. While many authors followed Doyle's lead by developing detectives who made regular appearances in their tales, some authors chose instead to develop a *criminal* who repeatedly plied his trade in various episodes.

In either case, careful observation and logical thinking brings all of these cases to a satisfying conclusion. Sometimes the law metes out judgment as seen in "The Lenton Croft Mystery"; sometimes the perpetrator brings loss upon himself as seen in "The Episode of the Diamond Links"; and in rare cases the detective extends mercy to someone who has hurt only himself as does the repentant thief in "The Adventure of the Blue Carbuncle."

This Fingerprint Classic brings together a collection of mysteries of varying styles that share a similar theme—jewel theft.

Contents

1

The Lenton Croft Mystery

by Arthur Morrison

At the head of the first flight of a dingy staircase leading up from an ever open portal in a street by the Strand stood a door, the dusty ground-glass upper panel of which carried in its center the single word "Hewitt," while at its right-hand lower corner, in smaller letters, "Clerk's Office" appeared. On a morning when the clerks in the ground floor offices had barely hung up their hats, a short, well-dressed young man, wearing spectacles, hastening to open the dusty door, ran into the arms of another man who suddenly issued from it.

"I beg pardon," the first said. "Is this Hewitt's Detective Agency Office?"

"Yes, I believe you will find it so," the other replied. He was a stout, clean-shaven man, of middle height, and of a cheerful, round countenance. "You'd better speak to the clerk."

In the little outer office the visitor was met by a sharp lad with inky fingers, who presented him with a pen and a printed slip. The printed slip having been filled with the visitor's name and present business, and conveyed through an inner door, the lad reappeared with an invitation to the private office. There, behind a writing table, sat the stout man himself, who had only just advised an appeal to the clerk.

"Good morning, Mr. Lloyd—Mr. Vernon Lloyd," he said affably, looking again at the slip. "You'll excuse my care to start even with my visitors. I must, you know. You come from Sir James Norris, I see."

"Yes; I am his secretary. I have only to ask you to go straight to Lenton Croft at once, if you can, on very important business. Sir James would have wired, but had not your precise address. Can you go by the next train? 11:30 is the first available from Paddington."

"Quite possibly. Do you know anything of the business?"

"It is a case of a robbery in the house, or rather, I fancy, of several robberies. Jewelry has been stolen from rooms occupied by visitors to the Croft. The first case occurred some months ago—nearly a year ago in fact. Last night there was another. But I think you had better get the details on the spot. Sir James has told me to telegraph if you are coming, so that he may meet you himself at the station; and I must hurry, as his drive to the station will be a rather long one. Do I take it you will go, Mr. Hewitt? Twyford is the station."

"Yes, I shall come, and by the 11:30. Are you going by that train yourself?"

"No, I have several things to attend to now that I am in town. Good morning; I shall wire at once."

Mr. Martin Hewitt locked the drawer of his table and sent his clerk for a cab.

At Twyford Station Sir James Norris was waiting with a dog-cart. Sir James was a tall, florid man of fifty or thereabout, known away from home as something of a county historian, and nearer his own parts as a great supporter of the hunt, and a gentleman much troubled with poachers. As soon as he and Hewitt had found one another, the baronet hurried the detective into his dog-cart. "We've something over seven miles to drive," he said, "and I can tell you all about this wretched business as we go. That is why I came for you myself, and alone."

Hewitt nodded.

"I have sent for you, as Lloyd probably told you, because of a robbery at my place last evening. It appears, as far as I can guess, to be one of three by the same hand, or by the same gang. Late yesterday afternoon—"

"Pardon me, Sir James," Hewitt interrupted, "but I think I must ask you to begin at the first robbery and tell me the whole tale in proper order. It makes things clearer and sets them in their proper shape."

"Very well. Eleven months ago, or thereabout, I had rather a large party of visitors, and among them Colonel Heath and Mrs. Heath—the lady being a relative of my own late wife. Colonel Heath has not been long retired, you know—used to be political resident in India. Mrs. Heath had a rather good stock of jewelry of one sort and another, about the most valuable piece being a bracelet set with a particularly fine pearl—quite an exceptional pearl, in fact—that had been one of a heap of presents from the maharajah of his state when Heath left India.

"It was a very noticeable bracelet, the gold setting being a mere featherweight piece of native filigree work—almost too fragile to trust on the wrist—and the pearl being, as I have said, of a size and quality not often seen. Well, Heath and his wife arrived late one evening, and after lunch the following day, most of the men being off by themselves—shooting, I think—my daughter, my sister who is very often down here, and Mrs. Heath took it into their heads to go walking—fern-hunting, and so on. My sister was rather long dressing, and while they waited, my daughter went into Mrs. Heath's room, where Mrs. Heath turned over all her treasures to show her, as women do, you know. When my sister was at last ready, they came straight away, leaving the things littered about the room rather than stay longer to pack them up. The bracelet, with other things, was on the dressing table then."

"One moment," said Hewitt. "As to the door?"

"They locked it. As they came away my daughter suggested turning the key, as we had one or two new servants about."

3

"And the window?"

"That they left open, as I was going to tell you. Well, they went on their walk and came back, with Lloyd, whom they had met somewhere, carrying their ferns for them. It was dusk and almost dinnertime. Mrs. Heath went straight to her room, and the bracelet was gone."

"Was the room disturbed?"

"Not a bit. Everything was precisely where it had been left, except the bracelet. The door hadn't been tampered with, but the window was open, as I have told you."

"You called the police, of course?"

"Yes, and had a man from Scotland Yard down in the morning. He seemed a pretty smart fellow, and the first thing he noticed on the dressing table, within an inch or two of where the bracelet had been, was a match, which had been lit and thrown down. Now nobody about the house had had occasion to use a match in that room that day, and if they had, certainly wouldn't have thrown it on the cover of the dressing table. So, presuming the thief to have used that match, the robbery must have been committed when the room was getting dark . . . immediately before Mrs. Heath returned, in fact. The thief had evidently struck the match, passed it hurriedly over the various trinkets lying about, and taken the most valuable."

"Nothing else was even moved?"

"Nothing at all. Then the thief must have escaped by the window, although it was not quite clear how. The walking party approached the house with a full view of the window, but saw nothing, although the robbery must have been actually taking place a moment or two before they turned up."

"There was no water pipe within the proximity of the window, but a ladder usually kept in the stable yard was found lying along the edge of the lawn. The gardener explained, however, that he had put the ladder there after using it himself early in the afternoon."

"Of course, Sir James, it might easily have been used again after that and put back."

"Just what the Scotland Yard man said. He was pretty sharp too, on the gardener, but very soon decided that he knew nothing of it. No stranger had been seen in the neighborhood nor had passed the lodge gates. Besides, as the detective said, it scarcely seemed the work of a stranger. A stranger could scarcely have known enough to go straight to the room, where a lady—only arrived the day before—had left a valuable jewel, and away again without being seen. So all the people about the house were suspected in turn. The servants offered, in a body, to have their boxes searched, and this was done; everything was turned over, from the butler's to the new kitchen maid's. I don't know that I should have had this carried quite so far if I had been the loser myself, but it was my guest, and I was in such a horrible position. Well, there's little more to be said about that, unfortunately. Nothing came of it all, and the thing's as great a mystery now as ever. I believed the Scotland Yard man got as far as suspecting *me* before he gave it up altogether, but give it up he did in the end. I think that's all I know about the first robbery. Is it clear?"

"Oh, yes; I shall probably want to ask a few questions when I have seen the place, but they can wait. What next?"

"Well," Sir James pursued, "the next was a very common affair, that I should have forgotten all about probably, if it hadn't been for one circumstance. Even now I hardly think it could have been the work of the same hand. Four months or so after Mrs. Heath's disaster in February of this year, Mrs. Armitage, a young widow, who had been a school fellow of my daughter's, stayed with us for a week or so. Mrs. Armitage is a very active young lady, and was scarcely in the house half an hour before she arranged a drive in a pony cart with Eva, my daughter, to look up old people in the village that she used to know before she was married. So they set off in the afternoon, and made such a round of it that they were late for dinner. Mrs. Armitage had a small plain gold brooch, not at all valuable, you know; two or three pounds, I suppose which she used to pin up a cloak or anything

5

of that sort. Before she went out she stuck this in the pincushion on her dressing table, and left a ring—rather a good one, I understand—lying close by."

"This," asked Hewitt, "was not in the room that Mrs. Heath had occupied, I take it?"

"No; this was in another part of the building. Well, the brooch was taken, evidently, by some one in quite a hurry, for when Mrs. Armitage got back to her room, there was the pincushion with a little tear in it where the brooch had been simply snatched off. But the curious thing was that the ring—worth a dozen of the brooch—was left where it had been put. Mrs. Armitage didn't remember whether or not she had locked the door herself, although she found it locked when she returned; but my niece, who was indoors all the time, went and tried it once—she remembered that a gas-fitter was at work on the landing near by—and found it safely locked. The gas-fitter, whom we didn't know at the time, but who since seems to be quite an honest fellow, was ready to swear that nobody but my niece had been to the door while he was in sight of it, which was almost all the time. As to the window, the sash-line had broken that very morning, and Mrs. Armitage had propped open the bottom half about eight or ten inches with a brush; and when she returned, that brush, sash, and all were exactly as she had left them. Now I scarcely need tell *you* what an awkward job it must have been for anybody to get noiselessly in at that unsupported window; and how unlikely he would have been to replace it, with the brush, exactly as he found it."

"Just so. I suppose the brooch was really gone? I mean, there was no chance of Mrs. Armitage having mislaid it?"

"Oh, none at all, Hewitt. There was a most careful search."

"Then, as to getting in at the window, would it have been easy?"

"Well, yes," Sir James replied, "yes, perhaps it would. It is a first floor window, and it looks over the roof and skylight of the billiard room. I built the billiard room myself. Built it just at this corner. It would be easy enough to get at the window from the billiard room roof. But then," he added, "that couldn't have been the way. Somebody or other was in the billiard room the whole time, and nobody could have got over the roof, which is nearly all skylight, without being seen and heard. I was there myself for an hour or two, taking a little practice."

"Well, was anything done?"

"Strict inquiry was made among the servants, of course, but nothing came of it. It was such a small matter that Mrs. Armitage wouldn't hear of my calling in the police or anything of that sort, although I felt pretty certain that there must be a dishonest servant about somewhere. A servant might take a *plain* brooch, you know, who would feel afraid of a valuable ring, the loss of which would be made a greater matter of."

"Well, yes, perhaps so, in the case of an inexperienced thief, who also would be likely to snatch up whatever she took in a hurry. But I'm doubtful. What made you connect these two robberies together?"

"Nothing whatever, for some months. They seemed quite of a different sort. But scarcely more than a month ago I met Mrs. Armitage at Brighton, and we talked, among other things, of the previous robbery, that of Mrs. Heath's bracelet. I described the circumstances pretty minutely, and when I mentioned the match found on the table, she said, 'How strange! Why, *my* thief left a match on the dressing table when he took my poor little brooch!' "

Hewitt nodded. "Yes," he said. "A spent match, of course?"

"Yes, of course, a spent match. She noticed it lying close by the pincushion, but threw it away without mentioning the circumstance. Still, it seemed rather curious to me that a match should be lit and dropped in each case, on the dressing cover an inch from where the article was taken. I mentioned it to Lloyd when I got back, and he agreed that it seemed significant."

"Scarcely," said Hewitt, shaking his head. "Scarcely, so far, to be called significant, although worth following up. Everybody uses matches in the dark, you know."

"Well, at any rate, the coincidence appealed to me so far that it struck me it might be worthwhile to describe the brooch to the police in order that they could trace it if it had been pawned. They had tried that, of course, over the bracelet without any result, but I fancied the shot might be worth making, and might possibly lead us on the track of the more serious robbery."

"Quite so. It was the right thing to do. Well?"

"Well, they found it. A woman had pawned it in London at a shop in Chelsea. But that was sometime before, and the pawnbroker had clean forgotten all about the woman's appearance. The name and address she gave were false. So that was the end of that business."

"Had any of your servants left you between the time the brooch was lost and the date on the pawn ticket? Were all your servants at home on the day the brooch was pawned?"

"Oh, yes! I made that inquiry myself."

"Very good! What next, Sir James?"

"Yesterday. And this is what made me send for you. My late wife's sister came here last Tuesday, and we gave her the room from which Mrs. Heath lost her bracelet. She had with her a very old-fashioned brooch, containing a miniature of her father, and set in front with three very fine brilliants and a few smaller stones. Here we are, though, at the Croft. I'll tell you the rest indoors."

Hewitt laid his hand on the baronet's arm. "Don't pull up, Sir James," he said. "Drive a little further. I should like to have a general idea of the whole case before we go in."

"Very good." Sir James Norris straightened the horse's head again and went on. "Late yesterday afternoon, as my sister-in-law was changing her dress, she left her room for a moment to speak to my daughter in her room, almost adjoining. She was gone no more than three minutes—five at the most. But when she returned, the brooch, which had been left on the table, was gone. Now the window was shut fast, and had not been tampered with. Of course the door was open, but so was my daughter's, and any-

8

body walking near must have been heard. But the strangest circumstance, and one that almost makes me wonder whether I have been awake today or not, was that there lay *a used match* on the very spot, as nearly as possible, where the brooch had been . . . and it was broad daylight!"

Hewitt rubbed his nose and looked thoughtfully before him. "Hmm. Curious, certainly," he said. "Anything else?"

"Nothing more than you shall see for yourself. I have had the room locked and watched till you could examine it. My sister-in-law had heard of your name and suggested that you should be called in; so, of course, I did exactly as she wanted. That she should have lost that brooch, of all things, in my house is most unfortunate; you see, there was some small difference about the thing between my late wife and her sister when their mother died and left it. It's almost worse than the Heaths' bracelet business, and altogether I'm not pleased with things, I can assure you. See what a position it is for me? Here are three ladies, in the space of one year, robbed one after another in this mysterious fashion in *my* house, and I can't find the thief! It's horrible! People will be afraid to come near the place. And I can do nothing."

"Ah, well, we'll see. Perhaps we had better turn back now. By the way, were you thinking of having any alterations or additions made to your house?"

"No. What makes you ask?"

"I think you might at least consider the question of painting and decorating, Sir James. Or, say, putting up another coach house, or something. Because I should like to be (to the servants) the architect—or the builder, if you please—come to look around. You haven't told any of them about this business?"

"Not a word. Nobody knows but my relatives and Lloyd. I took every precaution myself, at once. As to your little disguise, be the architect by all means, and do as you please. If you can only find this thief and put an end to this horrible state of affairs, you'll do me the greatest service I've ever asked for. And as to your fee, I'll gladly make it whatever is usual, and three hundred in addition."

Martin Hewitt bowed. "You're very generous, Sir James, and you may be sure I'll do what I can. As a professional man, of course, a good fee always stimulates my interest, although this case of yours certainly seems interesting enough by itself."

"Most extraordinary! Don't you think so? Here are three persons, all ladies, all in my house, two even in the same room, each successively robbed of a piece of jewelry, each from a dressing table, and a used match left behind in every case. All in the most difficult—one would say impossible—circumstances for a thief, and yet there is no clue."

"Well, we won't say that just yet, Sir James; we must see. And we must guard against any undue predisposition to consider the robberies in a lump. Here we are at the lodge gate again. Is that your gardener—the man who left the ladder by the lawn on the first occasion you spoke of?" Mr. Hewitt nodded in the direction of a man who was clipping a box border.

"Yes; will you ask him anything?"

"No, no; at any rate, not now. Remember the building alterations. I think, if there is no objection, I will look first at the room that the lady . . . Mrs. . . . ." Hewitt looked up enquiringly.

"My sister-in-law? Mrs. Cazenove. Oh, yes! You shall come to her room at once."

"Thank you. And I think Mrs. Cazenove had better be there."

They alighted, and a boy from the lodge led the horse and dogcart away.

Mrs. Cazenove was a thin and faded, but quick and energetic, lady of middle age. She bent her head very slightly on learning Martin Hewitt's name, and said, "I must thank you, Mr. Hewitt, for your very prompt attention. I need scarcely say that any help you can afford in tracing the thief who has my property—whoever it may be—will make me most grateful. My room is quite ready for you to examine."

The room was on the second floor—the top floor at that part of the building. Some slight confusion of small articles of dress was observable in parts of the room.

"This, I take it," inquired Hewitt, "is exactly as it was at the time the brooch was missed?"

"Precisely," Mrs. Cazenove answered. "I have used another room, and put myself to some other inconveniences, to avoid any disturbance."

Hewitt stood before the dressing table. "Then this is the used match," he observed, "exactly where it was found?"

"Yes."

"Where was the brooch?"

"I should say almost on the very same spot. Certainly no more than a very few inches away."

Hewitt examined the match closely. "It is burned very little," he remarked. "It would appear to have gone out at once. Could you hear it struck?"

"I heard nothing whatever, absolutely nothing."

"If you will step into Miss Norris's room now for a moment," Hewitt suggested, "we will try an experiment. Tell me if you hear matches struck, and how many. Where is the match stand?"

The match stand proved to be empty, but matches were found in Miss Norris's room, and the test was made. Each striking could be heard distinctly, even with one of the doors pushed to.

"Both your own door and Miss Norris's were open, I understand; the window shut and fastened inside as it is now, and nothing but the brooch was disturbed?"

"Yes, that was so."

"Thank you, Mrs. Cazenove. I don't think I need trouble you further just at present. I think, Sir James," Hewitt added, turning to the baronet, who was standing by the door, "I think we will see the other room and take a walk outside the house, if you please. I suppose, by the way, that there is no getting at the matches left behind on the first and second occasions?"

"No," Sir James answered. "Certainly not here. The Scotland Yard man may have kept his."

The room that Mrs. Armitage had occupied presented no peculiar feature. A few feet below the window the roof of the billiard room was visible, consisting largely of skylight. Hewitt glanced casually about the walls, ascertained that the furniture and hangings had not been materially changed since the second robbery, and expressed his desire to see the windows from the outside. Before leaving the room, however, he wished to know the names of any persons who were known to have been about the house on the occasions of all three robberies.

"Just carry your mind back, Sir James," he said. "Begin with yourself, for instance. Where were you at these times?"

"When Mrs. Heath lost her bracelet, I was in Tagley Wood all the afternoon. When Mrs. Armitage was robbed, I believe I was somewhere about the place most of the time she was out. Yesterday I was down at the farm." Sir James's face broadened. "I don't know whether you call those suspicious movements," he added, and laughed.

"Not at all; I only asked you so that, remembering your own movements, you might the better recall those of the rest of the household. Was anybody, to your knowledge—*anybody*, mind—in the house on all three occasions?"

"Well, you know, it's quite impossible to answer for all the servants. You'll only get that by direct questioning. I can't possibly remember things of that sort. As to the family and visitors . . . why, you don't suspect any of them, do you?"

"I don't suspect a soul, Sir James," Hewitt answered, beaming genially, "not a soul. You see, I *can't* suspect people till I know something about where they were. It's quite possible there will be independent evidence enough as it is, but you must help me if you can. The visitors, now. Was there any visitor here each time . . . or even on the first and last occasions only?"

"No, not one. And my own sister, perhaps you will be pleased to know, was only there at the time of the first robbery."

"Just so! And your daughter, as I have gathered, was clearly absent from the spot each time and indeed was in the company of the party robbed. Your niece, now?"

"Why, Mr. Hewitt, I can't talk of my niece as a suspected criminal! The poor girl's under my protection, and I really can't allow—"

Hewitt raised his hand and shook his head deprecatingly. "My dear sir, haven't I said that I don't suspect a soul? *Do* let me know how the people were distributed, as nearly as possible. Let me see. It was your niece, I think, who found that Mrs. Armitage's door was locked—this door, in fact—on the day she lost her brooch?"

"Yes, it was."

"Just so. At the time when Mrs. Armitage herself had forgotten whether she locked it or not. And yesterday? Was she out then?"

"No, I think not. Indeed, she goes out very little—her health is usually bad. She was indoors too, at the time of the Heath robbery, since you ask. But come now, I don't like this. It's ridiculous to suppose that she knows anything of it."

"I don't suppose it, as I have said. I am only asking for information. That is all your resident family I take it, and you know nothing of anybody else's movements except, perhaps, Mr. Lloyd's?"

"Lloyd? Well, you know yourself that he was out with the ladies when the first robbery took place. As to the others, I don't remember. Yesterday he was probably in his room writing, I think that acquits *him*, eh?"

Sir James looked quizzically into the broad face of the affable detective, who smiled and replied, "Of course nobody can be in two places at once, else what would become of the alibi as an institution? But, as I have said, I am only setting my facts in order. Now, you see, we get down to the servants, unless some stranger is the party wanted. Shall we go outside now?"

Lenton Croft was a large, haphazard sort of house, nowhere more than three floors high, and mostly only two. It had been added to bit by bit, till it zigzagged about its site, as Sir James Norris expressed it, "like a game of dominoes." Hewitt scrutinized its external features carefully as they strolled round, and stopped some little while before the windows of the two bedrooms he had just seen from the inside. Presently they approached the stables and coach house, where a groom was washing the wheels of the dogcart.

A smart little terrier was trotting about by the coach house, and Hewitt stopped to rub its head. Then he made some observation about the dog, which enlisted the groom's interest, and was soon absorbed in a chat with the man. Sir James, waiting a little way off, tapped the stones rather impatiently with his foot, and presently moved away.

For full a quarter of an hour Hewitt chatted with the groom, and, when at last he came away and overtook Sir James, the gentleman was about to reenter the house.

"I beg your pardon, Sir James," Hewitt said, "for leaving you in that unceremonious fashion to talk to your groom, but a dog, Sir James, a good dog, will draw me anywhere."

"Oh," replied Sir James shortly.

"There is one other thing," Hewitt went on, disregarding the other's curtness, "that I should like to know. There are two windows directly below that of the room occupied yesterday by Mrs. Cazenove—one on each floor. What rooms do they light?"

"That on the ground floor is the morning room; the other is Mr. Lloyd's—my secretary. A sort of study or sitting room."

"Now you will see at once, Sir James," Hewitt pursued, with an affable determination to win the baronet back to good humor, "you will see at once that, if a ladder had been used in Mrs. Heath's case, anybody looking from either of these rooms would have seen it."

"Of course. The Scotland Yard man questioned everybody as to that, but nobody seemed to have been in either of the rooms when the thing occurred; at any rate, nobody saw anything."

"Still, I think I should like to look out of those windows myself; it will, at least, give me an idea of what *was* in view and what was not, if anybody had been there."

Sir James Norris led the way to the morning room. As they reached the door a young lady, carrying a book and walking very languidly, came out. Hewitt stepped aside to let her pass, and afterward asked, "Miss Norris, your daughter, Sir John?"

"No, my niece. Do you want to ask her anything? Dora, my dear . . ." Sir James added, following her in the corridor, "this is Mr. Hewitt, who is investigating these wretched robberies for me. I think he would like to hear if you remember anything happening at any of the three times."

The lady bowed slightly, and said in a plaintive drawl, "I, uncle? Really, I don't remember anything; nothing at all."

"You found Mrs. Armitage's door locked, I believe," asked Hewitt, "when you tried it, on the afternoon when she lost her brooch?"

"Oh, yes; I believe it was locked. Yes, it was."

"Had the key been left in?"

"The key? No, I think not; no."

"Do you remember anything out of the common happening—anything whatever, no matter how trivial—on the day Mrs. Heath lost her bracelet?"

"No, really, I don't. I can't remember at all."

"Nor yesterday?"

"No, nothing. I don't remember anything."

"Thank you," said Hewitt hastily; "thank you. Now the morning room, Sir James."

In the morning room Hewitt stayed but a few seconds, doing little more than casually glance out of the windows. In the room above he took a little longer time. It was a comfortable room with little pieces of draped silk work hung about the furniture, and Japanese silk fans decorated the mantelpiece. Near the window was a cage containing a gray parrot, and the writing table was decorated with two vases of flowers.

"Lloyd makes himself pretty comfortable, eh?" Sir James observed. "But it isn't likely anybody would be here while he was out, at the time that bracelet went."

"No," replied Hewitt meditatively. "No, I suppose not."

He stared thoughtfully out of the window, and then, still deep in thought, rattled at the wires of the cage with a quill toothpick and played a moment with the parrot. Then, looking up at the window again, he said, "That is Mr. Lloyd, isn't it, coming back?"

"Yes, I think so. Is there anything else you would care to see here?"

"No, thank you," Hewitt replied; "I don't think there is."

They went down to the smoking room, and Sir James went away to speak to his secretary. When he returned, Hewitt said quietly. "I think, Sir James—I *think* that I shall be able to give you your thief presently."

"What! Have you a clue? Who do you think? I began to believe you were hopelessly stumped."

"Well, yes. I have rather a good clue, although I can't tell you much about it just yet. But it is so good a clue that I should like to know now whether you are determined to prosecute when you have the criminal?"

"Why, of course!" Sir James replied with surprise. "It doesn't rest with me, you know—the property belongs to my friends. And even if *they* were disposed to let the thing slide, I shouldn't allow it—I couldn't, after they had been robbed in my house."

"Of course, of course! Then, if I can, I should like to send a message to Twyford by somebody perfectly trustworthy—not a servant. Could anybody go?"

"Well, there's Lloyd, although he's only just back from his journey. But, if it's important, he'll go."

"It *is* important. The fact is we must have a policeman or two here this evening, and I'd like Mr. Lloyd to fetch them without telling anybody else."

Sir James rang, and in response to his message, Mr. Lloyd appeared. While Sir James gave his secretary his instructions, Hewitt strolled to the door of the smoking room, and intercepted the latter as he came out.

"I'm sorry to give you this trouble, Mr. Lloyd," he said, "but I must stay here myself for a little, and somebody who can be trusted must go. Will you just bring back a policeman with you? or rather two—two would be better. That is all that is wanted. You won't let the servants know, will you?" And, chatting thus confidentially, Martin Hewitt saw him off.

When Hewitt returned to the smoking room, Sir James said suddenly, "Why, bless my soul, Mr. Hewitt, we haven't fed you! I'm awfully sorry. We came in rather late for lunch, you know, and this business has bothered me so I clean forgot everything else. There's no dinner till seven, so you'd better let me give you something now. I'm really sorry. Come along!"

"Thank you, Sir James," Hewitt replied; "I won't take much. A few biscuits, perhaps, or something of that sort. And, by the way, if you don't mind, I rather think I should like to take it alone. The fact is I want to go over this case thoroughly by myself. Can you put me in a room?"

"Any room you like. Where will you go? The dining room's rather large, but there's my study, that's pretty snug, or—"

"Perhaps I can go into Mr. Lloyd's room for half-an-hour or so; I don't think he'll mind, and it's pretty comfortable."

"Certainly, if you'd like. I'll tell them to send you whatever they've got."

"Thank you very much. Perhaps they'll also send me a lump of sugar and a walnut; it's—it's just a little fad of mine!"

"A—what? A lump of sugar and a walnut?" Sir James stopped for a moment, with his hand on the bell rope. "Oh, certainly, if you'd like it; certainly," he added, and stared after this detective of curious tastes as he left the room.

When the vehicle bringing back the secretary and the policemen drew up on the drive, Martin Hewitt left the room on the first floor and proceeded downstairs. On the landing he met Sir James Norris and Mrs. Cazenove, who stared with astonishment on perceiving that the detective carried in his hand the parrot cage.

"I think our business is about brought to a head now," Hewitt remarked on the stairs. "Here are the police officers from Twyford." The men were standing in the hall with Mr. Lloyd, who, catching sight of the cage in Hewitt's hand, paled suddenly.

"This is the person who will be charged, I think," Hewitt pursued, addressing the officers, and indicating Lloyd with his finger.

"What, Lloyd?" gasped Sir James, "No—not Lloyd—nonsense!"

"He doesn't seem to think it nonsense himself, does he?" Hewitt placidly observed. Lloyd had sunk on a chair and, gray of face, was staring blindly at the man he had run against at the office door that morning. His lips moved in spasms, but there was no sound. The wilted flower fell from his buttonhole to the floor, but he did not move.

"This is his accomplice," Hewitt went on, placing the parrot and cage on the hall table, "though I doubt whether there will be any use in charging *him*. Eh, Polly?"

The parrot turned his head to the side and chuckled. "Hullo, Polly!" It quietly gurgled, "Come along!"

Sir James Norris was hopelessly bewildered. "Lloyd— Lloyd," he said, under his breath, "Lloyd . . . and the bird?"

"This was his little messenger, his useful Mercury," Hewitt explained, tapping the cage complacently; "in fact, the actual lifter. Hold him up!"

The last remark referred to the wretched Lloyd, who had fallen forward with something between a sob and a loud sigh. The policemen took him by the arms and propped him in his chair.

"System?" said Hewitt, with a shrug of the shoulders, an hour or two after in Sir James's study. "I can't say I have a system. I call it nothing but common sense and a sharp pair of eyes. Nobody using these could help taking the right road in this case. I began at the match, just as the Scotland Yard man did, but I had the advantage of taking a line through three cases. To begin with, it was plain that that match, being left there in daylight in Mrs. Cazenove's room, could not have been used to light the tabletop in the full glare of the window; therefore it had been used for some other purpose. *What* purpose I could not, at the moment, guess. Habitual thieves, you know, often have curious superstitions, and some will never take anything without leaving something behind—a pebble or a piece of coal, or something like that—in the premises they have been robbing. It seemed at first extremely likely that this was a case of that kind. The match had clearly been *brought in* because, when I asked for matches, there were none in the stand, not even an empty box, and the room had not been disturbed. Also the match probably had not been struck there, nothing having been heard, although, of course, a mistake in this matter was just possible. This match, then, it was fair to assume, had been lit somewhere else and blown out immediately— I remarked at the time that it was very little burned—with the only possible reason to prevent it igniting accidentally. Following this line of thought, it became obvious that the match was used, for whatever purpose, not *as* a match, but merely as a convenient splinter of wood.

"So far so good. But on examining the match very closely I observed, as you can see for yourself, certain rather sharp indentations in the wood. They are very small, you see, and scarcely visible, except upon narrow inspection; but there they are, and their positions are regular. See—there are two on each side, each opposite the corresponding mark of the other pair. The match, in fact, would seem to have been gripped in some fairly sharp instrument, holding it at two points above and two below—an instrument not unlike the beak of a bird.

"Now here was an idea. What living creature but a bird could possibly have entered Mrs. Heath's window without a ladder—supposing no ladder to have been used—or could have got into Mrs. Armitage's window without lifting the sash higher than the eight or ten inches it was already open? Plainly, nothing. Further, it is significant that only *one* article was stolen at a time, although others were about. A human being could have carried any reasonable number, but a bird could only take one at a time. But why should a bird carry a match in its beak? Certainly it must have been trained to do that for a purpose, and a little consideration made that purpose pretty clear. A noisy, chattering bird would probably betray itself at once. Therefore it must be trained to keep quiet both while going for and coming away with its plunder. What readier or more probably effectual way then, while teaching it to carry without dropping, to teach it also to keep quiet while carrying? The one thing would practically cover the other.

"I thought at once, of course, of a jackdaw or a magpie—these birds' thievish reputations made the guess natural. But the marks on the match were much too wide apart to have been made by the beak of either. I conjectured, therefore, that it must be a raven. So that, when we arrived near the coachhouse, I seized the opportunity of a little chat with your groom on the subject of dogs and pets in general, and ascertained that there was no tame raven in the place. I also ascertained that the match found was of the sort generally used about the establishment—the large, thick, red-topped English match. But I further found that Mr. Lloyd had a parrot, which was a most intelligent pet, and had been trained into comparative quietness—for a parrot. Also, I learned that more than once the groom had met Mr. Lloyd carrying his parrot under his coat, it having, as its owner explained, learned the trick of opening its cage door and escaping.

"I said nothing, of course, to you of all this, because I had as yet nothing but a train of argument and no results. I got to Lloyd's rooms as soon as possible. My chief object in going there was achieved when I played with the parrot, and induced it to bite a quill toothpick.

"When you left me in the smoking room, I compared the quill and the match very carefully, and found that the marks corresponded exactly. After this I felt very little doubt indeed. The fact that Lloyd met the ladies walking before dark on the day of the first robbery proved nothing. It was clear that the match had *not* been used to procure a light, so the robbery might as easily have taken place in daylight as not, if my conjectures were right and I felt no doubt that they *were* right. There could be no other explanation.

"When Mrs. Heath left her window open and her door shut, anybody climbing upon the open sash of Lloyd's high window could have put the bird upon the sill above. The match placed in the bird's beak for the purpose I have indicated, and struck first, in case by accident it should ignite by rubbing against something and startle the bird. This match would, of course, be dropped just where the object to be removed was taken up. As you know, in every case the match was found almost upon the spot where the missing article had been left—scarcely a likely triple coincidence had the match been used by a human thief. This would have been done as soon after the ladies had left as possible, and there would then have been plenty of time for Lloyd to hurry out and meet them before dark—especially plenty of time to meet them *coming back,* as they must have been, since they were carrying their ferns. The match was an article well chosen for its purpose, as being a not altogether unlikely thing to find on a dressing table, and if noticed, likely to lead to the wrong conclusions adopted by the official detective.

"In Mrs. Armitage's case the taking of an inferior brooch and the leaving of a more valuable ring pointed clearly either to the operator being a fool or unable to distinguish values, and certainly, from other indications, the thief seemed no fool. The door was locked, and the gas fitter, so to speak, on guard, and the window was only eight or ten inches open and propped with a brush.

A human thief entering the window would have disturbed this arrangement, and would scarcely risk discovery by attempting to replace it, especially a thief in so great a hurry as to snatch the brooch up without unfastening the pin. The bird could pass through the opening as it was, and *would have* to tear the pincushion to pull the brooch off, probably holding the cushion down with its claw the while.

"Now in yesterday's case we had an alteration of conditions. The window was shut and fastened, but the door was open—but only left for a few minutes, during which time no sound was heard either of coming or going. Was it not possible then, that the thief was *already* in the room, in hiding, while Mrs. Cazenove was there, and seized its first opportunity on her temporary absence? The room is full of draperies, hangings, and what not, allowing of plenty of concealment for a bird, and a bird could leave the place noiselessly and quickly. That the whole scheme was strange mattered not at all. Robberies presenting such unaccountable features must have been effected by strange means of one sort or another. There was no improbability—consider how many hundreds of examples of infinitely higher degrees of bird training are exhibited in the London streets every week for coppers.

"So that, on the whole, I felt pretty sure of my ground. But before taking any definite steps I resolved to see if Polly could not be persuaded to exhibit his accomplishments to an indulgent stranger. For that purpose I contrived to send Lloyd away again and have a quiet hour alone with his bird. A piece of sugar, as everybody knows, is a good parrot bribe; but a walnut, split in half, is a better—especially if the bird be used to it; so I got you to furnish me with both. Polly was shy at first, but I generally get along very well with pets, and a little perseverance soon led to a complete private performance for my benefit. Polly would take the match, mute as wax, jump on the table, pick up the brightest thing he could see in a great hurry, leave the match behind, and scuttle away round the room; but at first wouldn't give up the plunder to *me*. It was enough. I also took the liberty, as you know, of a general look round, and discovered that little collection of

Brummagem rings and trinkets that you have just seen—used in Polly's education, no doubt.

"When we sent Lloyd away, it struck me that he might as well be usefully employed as not, so I got him to fetch the police. There will be no trouble about evidence; he'll confess. Of that I am sure. I know the sort of man. But I doubt if you'll get Mrs. Cazenove's brooch back. You see, he has been to London today, and the piece is probably gone."

Sir James listened to Hewitt's explanation with many expressions of assent and some of surprise. When it was over, he said, "But Mrs. Armitage's brooch was pawned, and by a woman."

"Exactly. I expect our friend Lloyd was rather disgusted at his small fortune—probably gave the brooch to some female connection in London, and she capitalized on it. Such persons don't always trouble to give a correct address."

The two stood in silence for a few minutes, and then Hewitt continued, "I don't expect our friend has had an easy job altogether with that bird. His successes at most have only been three, and I suspect he had many failures and not a few anxious moments that we know nothing of. I should judge as much merely from what the groom told me of frequently meeting Lloyd with his parrot. But the plan was not a bad one—not at all. Even if the bird had been caught in the act, it would only have been *That mischievous parrot!* you see. And his master would only have been looking for him."

About the Author

Arthur Morrison (1863-1945) was born in Kent, England. He worked briefly in civil service and then turned his attentions to journalism.

He was both a novelist and a short story writer. He wrote several collections of stories about the investigator, Martin Hewitt. "The Lenton Croft Mystery" is the first story featuring Martin Hewitt and appeared in The Strand *in March 1894.*

2

The Azteck Opal

by Rodrigues Ottolengui

"Do sit down, Mr. Barnes." Mr. Mitchel indicated the tweed armchair with a sweep of his hand.

"Thank you, Mr. Mitchel. In a moment," said the detective. He paced over to the window and leaned an elbow on the sill, facing his friend with an expression of triumph. "Mr. Mitchel," he began, "I have called to see you upon a subject which I am sure will enlist your keenest interest . . . for several reasons. It relates to a magnificent jewel; it concerns your intimate friends; and it is a problem requiring the most analytical qualities of the mind in its solution."

"Ah! Then *you* have solved it?" asked Mr. Mitchel.

"I think so. You shall judge. I have today been called in to investigate one of the most singular cases that has fallen in my way. It is one in which the usual detective methods would be utterly valueless. The facts were presented to me, and the solution of the mystery could only be reached by analytical deduction."

"That is to say, by using your brains?"

"Precisely! Now, you have admitted that you consider yourself more expert in this direction than the ordinary detective. I wish to place you for once in the position of a detective, and then see you prove your ability."

The Azteck Opal

Mr. Mitchel settled back in his chair. "Present the case, then."
A smile twitched at the corner of his mouth. "I shall do my best."

Mr. Barnes cleared his throat and paced over to the fireplace.
He rested one hand on the mantel. "Early this morning I was sum-
moned, by a messenger, to go aboard of the steam yacht *Idler*,
which lay at anchor in the lower bay."

"Why, the *Idler* belongs to my friend Mortimer Gray," said
Mr. Mitchel.

"Yes," replied Mr. Barnes. "I told you that your friends are interested. I went immediately with the man who had come to my
office, and in due season I was taken aboard the yacht. Mr. Gray
received me very politely, and took me to his private room adjoining the cabin. Here he explained to me that he had been off
on a cruise for a few weeks, and was approaching the harbor last
night, when, in accordance with his plans, a sumptuous dinner
was served, as a sort of farewell feast, the party expecting to leave
today."

"What guests were on the yacht?"

"Patience." Mr. Barnes held up a hand. "I will tell you everything in order, as the facts were presented to me." He lowered
himself into the chair but sat forward, studying the rich pattern on
the Oriental rug. "Mr. Gray enumerated the party as follows. Besides himself and his wife, there were his wife's sister, Mrs. Eugene Cortlandt, and her husband, a Wall Street broker. Also, Mr.
Arthur Livingstone, and his sister, and a Mr. Dermett Moore, a
young man supposed to be devoting himself to Miss Livingstone."

Mr. Mitchel nodded. "That makes seven persons, three of
whom are women. I ought to say, Mr. Barnes, that, though Mr.
Gray is a club friend, I am not personally acquainted with his
wife, nor with the others. So I have no advantage over you."

"I will come at once to the curious incident which made my
presence desirable," said Mr. Barnes. "According to Mr. Gray's
story, the dinner had proceeded as far as the roast, when suddenly
there was a slight shock as the yacht touched a sandbar, and at the

25

same time the lamps spluttered and then went out, leaving the room totally dark. A second later the vessel righted herself and sped on, so that before any panic ensued, it was evident to all that the danger had passed. The gentlemen begged the ladies to resume their seats and remain quiet until the lamps were relighted; this, however, the attendants were unable to do, and they were ordered to bring fresh lamps. Thus there was almost total darkness for several minutes."

Mr. Mitchel closed his eyes and rubbed his forehead briefly. "During which, I presume, the person who planned the affair readily consummated his design?"

"So you think that the whole series of events was pre-arranged? Be that as it may, something did happen in that dark room. The women had started from their seats when the yacht touched, and when they groped their way back in the darkness some of them found the wrong places, as was seen when the fresh lamps were brought. This was considered a good joke, and there was some laughter, but this was suddenly checked by an exclamation from Mr. Gray, who quickly asked his wife, 'Where is your opal?' "

Mr. Mitchel's eyes flew open. "Her opal?" he asked, in tones which showed that his greatest interest was now aroused. "Do you mean, Mr. Barnes, that she was wearing the Azteck opal?"

"Oh! You know the gem?"

"I know nearly all gems of great value; but what of this one?" Mr. Mitchel leaned forward slightly.

"Mrs. Gray and her sister, Mrs. Cortlandt, had both donned evening gowns for this occasion, and Mrs. Gray had worn this opal as a pendant to a thin gold chain which hung round her neck. At Mr. Gray's question, all looked towards his wife, and it was noted that the clasp was open, and the opal missing. Of course it was supposed that it had merely fallen to the floor, and a search was immediately instituted. But the opal could not be found."

"That is certainly a very significant fact," said Mr. Mitchel. "But was the search thorough?"

"I should say *extremely* thorough, when we consider it was not conducted by a detective, who is supposed to be an expert in such matters. Mr. Gray described to me what was done, and he seems to have taken every precaution. He sent the attendants out of the salon, and he and his guests systematically examined every part of the room."

"Except the place where the opal really was concealed, you mean."

Mr. Barnes smiled wryly. "With that exception, of course, since they did not find the jewel. Not satisfied with this search by lamplight, Mr. Gray locked the salon, so that no one could enter it during the night, and another investigation was made in the morning."

Mr. Mitchel raised an eyebrow. "The pockets of the seven persons present were not examined, I presume?"

"No! I asked Mr. Gray why this had been omitted, and he said that it was an indignity which he could not possibly show to a guest." Mr. Barnes's voice assumed a confidential tone. "As you have asked this question, Mr. Mitchel, it is only fair for me to tell you that when I spoke to Mr. Gray on the subject he seemed very much confused. Nevertheless, however unwilling he may have been to search those of his guests who are innocent, he emphatically told me that if I had reasonable proof that anyone present had purloined the opal, he wished that individual to be treated as any other thief, without regard to gender or social position."

"One can scarcely blame him, because that opal was worth a fabulous sum," said Mr. Mitchel with a sigh. "I have myself offered Gray twenty-five thousand dollars for it, which was refused. This opal is one of the eyes of an Azteck idol, and if the other could be found, the two would be as interesting as any jewels in the world."

"That is the story which I was asked to unravel," continued Mr. Barnes, "and I must now relate to you what steps I have taken towards that end. It appears that, because of the loss of the jewels, no person has left the yacht, although no restraint was placed upon anyone by Mr. Gray. All knew, however, that he had sent for a detective, and it was natural that no one should offer to go until formally dismissed by the host. My plan, then, was to have a private interview with each of the seven persons who had been present at the dinner."

"Then you exempted the attendants from your suspicions?"

"I did. There was but one way by which one of the servants could have stolen the opal, and this was prevented by Mr. Gray. It was possible that the opal had fallen on the floor, and, though not found at night, a servant might have discovered and have appropriated it on the following morning, had he been able to enter the salon. But Mr. Gray had locked the doors. No servant, however bold, would have been able to take the opal from the lady's neck." He lifted his chin and regarded his friend with a confident air.

Mr. Mitchel nodded approvingly. "I think your reasoning is good, and so we will confine ourselves to the original seven."

"After my interview with Mr. Gray, I asked to have Mrs. Gray sent in to me. She came in, and at once I noted that she placed herself on the defensive. Women frequently adopt that manner with a detective." A frown creased his forehead. "Her story was very brief. The main point was that she was aware of the theft before the lamps were relighted. In fact, she felt someone's arms steal around her neck and knew when the opal was taken. I asked why she had made no outcry, and whether she suspected any special person. To these questions she replied that she supposed it was merely a joke perpetrated in the darkness, and therefore had made no resistance."

"She suspected no one in particular as the jokester, then?"

"She would not name anyone as suspected by her, but she was willing to tell me that the arms were bare, as she detected when they touched her neck." He cleared his throat. "I must say here, that although Miss Livingstone's dress was not cut low in the neck, it was, practically, sleeveless; and Mrs. Cortlandt's dress had no sleeves at all."

Mr. Mitchel nodded again but made no comment.

"One other significant statement made by this lady was that her husband had mentioned to her your offer of twenty-five thousand dollars for the opal, and had urged her to permit him to sell it, but she had refused."

Mr. Mitchel rose suddenly. "So! It was Madam that would not sell." He rubbed his chin with his hand, staring at the fire. "The plot thickens!" He walked over and prodded at a log with the poker. Then he returned to his chair and eased himself down, still watching the flames.

"You will observe, of course, the point about the naked arms of the thief," continued Mr. Barnes. "I therefore sent for Mrs. Cortlandt next. She had a curious story to tell. Unlike her sister, she was quite willing to express her suspicions. Indeed, she plainly intimated that she supposed that Mr. Gray himself had taken the jewel. I will endeavor to repeat her words." He glanced up toward the ceiling.

" 'Mr. Barnes,' said she, 'the affair is very simple. Gray is a miserable old skinflint. A Mr. Mitchel, an eccentric who collects gems, offered to buy that opal, and he has been bothering my sister for it ever since. When the lamps went out, he took the opportunity to steal it. I do not think this, I *know* it. How? Well, on account of the confusion and darkness, I sat in my sister's seat when I returned to the table. This explains his mistake, but he put his arms round my neck, and deliberately felt for the opal. I did not understand his purpose at the time, but now it is very evident.'

" 'Yes, madam,' said I, 'but how do you know it was Mr. Gray?'

" 'Why, I grabbed his hand, and before he could pull it away I felt the large cameo ring on his little finger. Oh, there is no doubt whatever.'

"I asked her whether Mr. Gray had his sleeves rolled up, and though she could not understand the purport of the question, she said 'No.' "

Mr. Mitchel stroked his mustache. "Most interesting," he murmured. "And you questioned Miss Livingstone next, I presume?"

"Yes, I had Miss Livingstone come in. She is a slight, tremulous young lady, who cries at the slightest provocation. During the interview, brief as it was, it was only by the greatest diplomacy that I avoided a scene of hysterics. She tried very hard to convince me that she knew absolutely nothing. She had not left her seat during the disturbance; of that she was sure. So how could she know anything about it? I asked her to name the one whom she thought might have taken the opal, and at this her agitation reached such a climax that I was obliged to let her go."

Mr. Mitchel's lips twitched at the corner. "You gained very little from her, I should say."

"In a case of this kind, Mr. Mitchel, where the criminal is surely one of a very few persons, we cannot fail to gain something from each person's story. A significant feature here was that though Miss Livingstone assures us that she did not leave her seat, she was sitting in a different place when the lamps were lighted again."

"That might mean anything or nothing."

"Exactly! But we are not deducing values yet." Mr. Barnes hurried on with his account. "Mr. Dermett Moore came to me next, and he is a straightforward, honest man if I ever saw one. He declared that the whole affair was a great mystery to him, and that, while ordinarily he would not care anything about it, he could not but be somewhat interested because he thought that one of the ladies, he would not say which one, suspected him. Mr. Livingstone also impressed me favorably. He declined to name the person suspected by him, though he admitted that he could do so. He made this significant remark:

" 'You are a detective of experience, Mr. Barnes, and ought to be able to decide which man amongst us could place his arms around Mrs. Gray's neck without causing her to cry out. But if your imagination fails you, suppose you enquire into the financial standing of all of us, and see which one would be most likely to profit by thieving? Ask Mr. Cortlandt.' "

Mr. Mitchel leaned back in his chair and placed his palms together. "Evidently Mr. Livingstone knows more than he tells."

"Yet he told enough for one to guess his suspicions, and to understand the delicacy which prompted him to say no more," said Mr. Barnes. "He, however, gave me a good point upon which to question Mr. Cortlandt. When I asked that gentleman if any of the men happened to be in pecuniary difficulties, he became grave at once. I will give you his answer.

" 'Mr. Livingstone and Mr. Moore are both exceedingly wealthy men,' he informed me, 'and I am a millionaire, in very satisfactory business circumstances at present. But I am very sorry to say that, though our host, Mr. Gray, is also a distinctly rich man, he has met with some reverses recently, and I can conceive that ready money would be useful to him. But for all that, it is preposterous to believe what your question evidently indicates. None of the persons in this party is a thief, and least of all could we suspect Mr. Gray. I am sure that if he wished his wife's opal, she would give it to him cheerily. No, Mr. Barnes, the opal is in some crack, or crevice, which we have overlooked. It is lost—not stolen.' "

Mr. Mitchel gazed at the detective. "And thus ended your interviews?"

"That ended the interviews with the several persons present, but I made one or two other inquiries, from which I elicited at least two significant facts. First, it was Mr. Gray himself who had indicated the course by which the yacht was steered last night, and which ran her over a sandbar. Second, someone had nearly emptied the oil from the lamps, so that they would have burned out in a short time, even if the yacht had not touched."

Mr. Mitchel was silent for a moment. "These, then, are your facts? And from these you have solved the problem?" He leaned forward and placed his chin in his hand. "Well then, Mr. Barnes, who stole the opal?"

Mr. Barnes shook his head. "Mr. Mitchel, I have told you all I know, but I wish you to work out a solution before I reveal my own opinion."

"I have already done so, Mr. Barnes." Mr. Mitchel reached into his shirt pocket and withdrew a scrap of paper. He strode over to the writing table and took up the pen with a flourish. "Here! I will write my suspicion on a bit of paper. . . ." He returned the paper to his pocket and wheeled around, facing Mr. Barnes. "So! Now tell me yours, and you shall know mine afterwards."

Mr. Barnes regarded him evenly. "Why, to my mind it is very simple. Mr. Gray, failing to obtain the opal from his wife by fair means, resorted to a trick. He removed the oil from the lamps, and charted out a course for his yacht which would take her over a sandbar, and when the opportune moment came, he stole the jewel. His actions since then have been merely to cover his crime, by shrouding the affair with mystery. By insisting upon a thorough search, and even sending for a detective, he makes it impossible for those who were present to accuse him hereafter. Undoubtedly Mr. Cortlandt's opinion will be the one generally adopted. Now what do you think?"

Mr. Mitchel crossed the room and retrieved his hat from the hat rack. "I think I will go with you at once and board the yacht *Idler*."

Mr. Barnes rose quickly and took a step forward, frowning. "But you have not told me whom you suspect," he said.

Mr. Mitchel brushed a speck of dust from his hat and placed it on his head. "Oh. That's immaterial," he said calmly. He thrust an arm into his coat. "I do not suspect Mr. Gray, so if you are correct you will have shown better ability than I." He seized his gloves and headed for the door. "Come! Let us hurry!"

Mr. Barnes grabbed his coat with an exasperated sigh.

Mr. Mitchel turned at the first corner and strode quickly toward the dock. "The steam launch is waiting to return you to the yacht, I presume?" He pointed to the launch.

"Yes, but—"

"We will take that, then."

Mr. Barnes quickened his pace to keep up. "Mr. Mitchel," he panted, "you will note that Mrs. Cortlandt alluded to you as 'an eccentric who collects gems.'"

Mr. Mitchel grunted in reply.

"I must admit that I have myself harbored a great curiosity as to your reasons for purchasing jewels which are valued beyond a mere conservative commercial price. Would you mind explaining why you began your collection?"

"I seldom explain my motives to others, especially when they relate to my more important pursuits in life." Mr. Mitchel walked several more paces in silence. Then he glanced over at Mr. Barnes with the twitch of a smile playing about his lips. "But in view of all that has passed between us, I think your curiosity justifiable, and I will gratify it. To begin with, I am a very wealthy man. I inherited great riches, and I have made a fortune myself. Have you any conception of the difficulties which harass a man of means?"

"Perhaps not in minute detail," said Mr. Barnes, "though I can guess that the lot of the rich is not as free from care as the pauper thinks it is."

"The point is this: the difficulty with a poor man is to get rich, while with the rich man the greatest trouble is to prevent the increase of his wealth. Some men, of course, make no effort in that direction, and those men are a menace to society. My own idea of the proper use of a fortune is to manage it for the benefit of others, as well as one's self, and especially to prevent its increase."

Mr. Barnes eyebrows rose. "And is it so difficult to do this? Cannot money be spent without limit?"

"Yes." Mr. Mitchel looked steadily ahead. "But unlimited evil follows such a course. This is sufficient to indicate to you that I am ever in search of a legitimate means of spending my income, provided that I may do good thereby."

The two men had reached the dock. Mr. Mitchel waited until they had boarded the launch and positioned themselves at the rail before continuing. "If I can do this, and at the same time afford myself pleasure, I claim that I am making the best use of my money." He stared out at the gray water. "Now I happen to be so constructed, that the most interesting studies to me are social problems, and of these I am most entertained with the causes and environments of crime. Such a problem as the one you brought to me today is of immense attractiveness to me, because the environment is one which is commonly supposed to preclude rather than to invite crime. Yet we have seen that despite the wealth of all concerned, someone has stooped to the commonest of crimes—theft."

Mr. Barnes glanced quickly around and spoke with lowered voice. "But what has this to do with your collection of jewels?"

Mr. Mitchel turned an intense gaze on the detective. "Everything! Jewels—especially those of great magnitude—seem to be a special cause of crime." He swept a hand toward the rocky coastline. "A hundred-carat diamond will tempt a man to theft, as surely as the false beacon on a rocky shore entices the mariner to wreck and ruin. All the great jewels of the world have murder and crime woven into their histories."

"All of them?"

"Every one. My attention was first called to this by accidentally overhearing a plot in a ballroom to rob the lady of the house of a large ruby which she wore on her breast. I went to her, taking the privilege of an intimate friend, and told her enough to persuade her to sell the stone to me. I fastened it into my scarf, and then sought the presence of the plotters, allowing them to see what had occurred. No words passed between us, but by my act I prevented a crime that night."

"Then am I to understand that you buy jewels with that end in view?"

Mr. Mitchel's eyes gleamed. "After that night, Barnes, I conceived this idea. If all the great jewels in the world could be collected together, and put in a place of safety, hundreds of crimes would be prevented, even before they had been imagined. Moreover, the search for, and acquirement of these jewels would necessarily afford me abundant opportunity for studying the crimes which are perpetrated in order to gain possession of them. Thus you understand more thoroughly why I am anxious to pursue this problem of the Azteck opal."

Several hours later Mr. Mitchel and Mr. Barnes were sitting at a quiet table in the corner of the dining room at Mr. Mitchel's club. "Mr. Mitchel, must you keep me in suspense?" asked Mr. Barnes in a low tone. "You acted quite mysteriously on board the yacht—closeting yourself with Mr. Gray, after which you interviewed two or three of the others. I was beginning to feel quite neglected, waiting alone on deck."

Mr. Mitchel smiled with satisfaction. "In light of your previous conjectures, you must have been surprised to see me appear arm in arm with Mr. Gray."

"Indeed so. And when I saw him hand you the envelope and heard him speak of remunerating you for your services with the enclosed check, I was very much tempted to protest."

Mr. Mitchel leaned back and let out a deep chuckle. "My dear Mr. Barnes, if I had not taken your arm and hurried you off in the cab, I fear you would have created quite a scene."

Mr. Barnes' face reddened. "I *am* entitled to an explanation, would you not agree?"

Mr. Mitchel only replied, "All in good time. I am too hungry to talk now. We will have dinner first."

The dinner was over at last, and nuts and coffee were before them, when Mr. Mitchel took a small parcel from his pocket, and handed it to Mr. Barnes, saying, "It is a beauty, is it not?"

When Mr. Barnes removed the tissue paper, a large opal fell on the tablecloth, where it sparkled with a thousand colors under the electric lamps.

The detective barely stifled a cry of surprise. He shielded the gem from the light with his hands and stared at Mr. Mitchel. "Do you mean that this is—"

"The Azteck opal, and the finest harlequin I ever saw," interrupted Mr. Mitchel. "But you wish to know how it came into my possession? Principally so that it may join the collection and cease to be a temptation to this world of wickedness."

"Then Mr. Gray did not steal it?" asked Mr. Barnes, with a touch of chagrin in his voice.

"No, Mr. Barnes. Mr. Gray did not steal it." Mr. Mitchel took a swallow of coffee and sighed with contentment. "But you are not to consider yourself very much at fault. Mr. Gray *tried* to steal it, only he failed. That was not your fault, of course. You read his actions aright, but you did not give enough weight to the stories of the others."

"What important point did I omit from my calculation?"

"I might mention the bare arms which Mrs. Gray said she felt round her neck. It was evidently Mr. Gray who looked for the opal on the neck of his sister-in-law, but as he did not bare his arms, he would not have done so later."

Mr. Barnes's eyes widened. "Do you mean that Miss Livingstone was the thief?"

Mr. Mitchel smiled. "No! Miss Livingstone being hysterical, she changed her seat without realizing it, but that does not make her a thief. Her excitement when with you was due to her suspicions, which, by the way, were correct." He replaced his cup on its saucer and pushed it to one side. "But let us return for a moment to the bare arms. That was the clue from which I worked. It was evident to me that the thief was a man, and it was equally plain that in the hurry of the few moments of darkness, no man would have rolled up his sleeves, risking the return of the attendants with lamps, and the consequent discovery of himself in such a singular disarrangement of costume."

"Then how do you account for the bare arms?"

The Azteck Opal

"The lady did not tell the truth. That is all. The arms which encircled her neck were not bare. Neither were they unknown to her. She told you that bit to shield the thief. She also told you that her husband wished to sell the Azteck opal to me, but that she had refused. Thus she deftly led you to suspect him. Now, if she wished to shield the thief, yet was willing to accuse her husband, it followed that the husband was not the thief."

"Very well reasoned, Mr. Mitchel. I see now where you are tending, but I shall not get ahead of your story."

Mr. Mitchel cracked a nut and crunched it leisurely before continuing. "So much I had deduced, before we went on board the yacht. When I found myself alone with Gray, I candidly told him of your suspicions, and your reasons for harboring doubt. He was very much disturbed, and pleadingly asked me what I thought. I told him frankly that I believed that he had tried to take the opal from his wife—we can scarcely call it stealing since the law does not—but that I believed he had failed."

"And what did he say to that?"

"He confessed; admitted emptying the lamps, but denied running the boat on the sandbar. But he assured me that he had not reached his wife's chair when the lamps were brought in. He was, therefore, much astonished at missing the gem. I promised him to find the jewel upon condition that he would sell it to me. To this he most willingly agreed."

"But how could you be sure that you would recover the opal?"

Mr. Mitchel looked somewhat amused by the question. "Partly by my knowledge of human nature, and partly because of my inherent faith in my own abilities. I sent for Mrs. Gray."

"And did you note her attitude of defense?"

"I did; however, it only satisfied me the more that I was right in my suspicions. I began by asking her if she knew the origin of the superstition that an opal brings bad luck to its owner. She did not, of course, comprehend my tactics, but she added that she 'had heard the stupid superstition, but took no interest in such nonsense.' I then gravely explained to her that the opal is the engagement stone of the Orient. The lover gives it to his sweetheart, and the belief is that should she deceive him even in the most trifling manner, the opal will lose its brilliancy and become cloudy." He met Mr. Barnes's eyes. "I then asked her if she had ever noted a change in her opal.

"She was immediately angry. 'What do you mean to insinuate?' she cried out.

" 'I mean,' said I, sternly, 'that if an opal has changed color in accordance with the superstition this one should have done so. I mean that though your husband greatly needs the money which I have offered him you have refused to allow him to sell it, and yet you have permitted another to take it from you tonight. By this act you might have seriously injured, if not ruined Mr. Gray. Why have you done it?' "

Mr. Barnes's eyes sparkled with admiration at his friend's ingenuity. "How did she receive it?" he asked.

"She began to sob, and between her tears she admitted that the opal had been taken by the man I suspected, but she earnestly declared that she had harbored no idea of injuring her husband. Indeed, she was so agitated in speaking upon this point, that I believe that Gray never thoroughly explained to her why he wished to sell the gem. She urged me to recover the opal if possible, and purchase it, so that her husband might be relieved from his pecuniary embarrassment."

"And then?"

"I then sent for the thief." As he spoke, Mr. Mitchel reached into his shirt pocket. "Mrs. Gray told me his name, but would you not like to hear how I had picked him out before we went aboard? I still have that bit of paper upon which I wrote his name, in confirmation of what I say." He passed the scrap to Mr. Barnes.

Mr. Barnes read the name scribbled on the slip of paper. "Of course," he said. "I know now that you mean Mr. Livingstone. But what were your reasons for suspecting him?"

Mr. Mitchel took another sip of coffee and settled back in his chair. "From your account Miss Livingstone suspected someone, and this caused her to be so agitated that she was unaware of the fact that she had changed her seat. Women are shrewd in these affairs, and I was confident that the girl had good reason for her conduct. It was evident that the person in her mind was either her brother or her sweetheart. I decided between these two men from your account of your interviews with them. Moore impressed you as being honest, and he told you that one of the ladies suspected him. In this he was mistaken, but his speaking to you of it was not the act of a thief. Mr. Livingstone, on the other hand, tried to throw suspicion upon Mr. Gray."

"Uhmm." Mr. Barnes murmured his assent. "Of course that was sound reasoning after you had concluded that Mrs. Gray was lying. Now tell me how you recovered the jewel?"

"That was easier than I expected. I simply told Mr. Livingstone when I got him alone, what I knew and asked him to hand me the opal. With a perfectly imperturbable manner, understanding that I promised secrecy, he quietly took it from his pocket and gave it to me, saying, 'Women are very poor conspirators. They are too weak.'"

"What did you tell Mr. Gray?"

"Oh, he did not inquire too closely into what I told him. My check was what he most cared for. I told him nothing definitely, but I implied that his wife had secreted the gem during the darkness, that he might not ask her for it again; and that she had intended to find it again at a future time, just as he had meant to pawn it and then pretend to recover it from the thief by offering a reward."

Mr. Barnes leaned forward. "One more question. Why did Mr. Livingstone steal it?"

"Ah!" Mr. Mitchel stared hard into the flame of the candle before him. "The truth about that is another mystery worth probing, and one which I shall make it my business to unravel. I will venture two prophecies. First—Mr. Livingstone did not steal it at all. Mrs. Gray simply handed it to him in the darkness. There must have been some powerful motive to lead her to such an act; something which she was weighing, and decided impulsively. This brings me to the second point. Livingstone used the word *conspirator*, which is a clue. You will recall what I told you, that this gem is one of a pair of opals, and that with the other, the two would be as interesting as any jewels in the world. I am confident now that Mr. Livingstone knows where that other opal is, and that he has been urging Mrs. Gray to give or lend him hers, as a means of obtaining the other. If she hoped to do this, it would be easy to understand why she refused to permit the sale of the one she had."

Mr. Barnes was silent, taking it all in.

Mr. Mitchel pushed back from the table and leaned to retrieve his hat from the empty chair. "This, of course, is guesswork." He stood and placed his hat at a jaunty angle, covering one eyebrow. His lips twitched slightly as he fixed a steady gaze on Mr. Barnes. "But I'll promise that if any one ever owns both opals, it shall be your humble servant, Leroy Mitchel, Jewel Collector."

About the Author

Rodrigues Ottolengui, 1861-1937, was born in Charleston, South Carolina. His parents were writers, and his paternal grandfather was a dentist. Ottolengui followed both paths finding success as a dentist and a writer. He was also an editor, an artist, a sculptor, and an expert in butterfly and moth collecting.

He read detective stories to improve his own analytical abilities and ultimately wrote six novels and a number of stories in the mystery genre. "The Azteck Opal" first appeared in April of 1895 in The Idler.

3

The Adventure of the Blue Carbuncle

by Sir Arthur Conan Doyle

I had called upon my friend Sherlock Holmes upon the second morning after Christmas, with the intention of wishing him the compliments of the season. He was lounging upon the sofa in a purple dressing-gown, a pipe-rack within his reach upon the right, and a pile of crumpled morning papers, evidently newly studied, near at hand. Beside the couch was a wooden chair, and on the angle of the back hung a very seedy and disreputable hard-felt hat, much the worse for wear, and cracked in several places. A lens and a forceps lying upon the seat of the chair suggested that the hat had been suspended in this manner for the purpose of examination.

"You are engaged," said I. "Perhaps I interrupt you."

"Not at all. I am glad to have a friend with whom I can discuss my results. The matter is a perfectly trivial one"—he jerked his thumb in the direction of the old hat—"but there are points in connection with it which are not entirely devoid of interest and even of instruction."

I seated myself in his armchair and warmed my hands before his crackling fire, for a sharp frost had set in, and the windows were thick with the ice crystals. "I suppose," I remarked, "that, homely as it looks, this thing has some deadly story linked on to it—that it is the clue which will guide you in the solution of some mystery and the punishment of some crime."

"No, no. No crime," said Sherlock Holmes, laughing. "Only one of those whimsical little incidents which will happen when you have four million human beings all jostling each other within the space of a few square miles. Amid the action and reaction of so dense a swarm of humanity, every possible combination of events may be expected to take place, and many a little problem will be presented which may be striking and bizarre without being criminal. We have already had experience of such."

"So much so," I remarked, "that of the last six cases which I have added to my notes, three have been entirely free of any legal crime."

"Precisely. You allude to my attempt to recover the Irene Adler papers, to the singular case of Miss Mary Sutherland, and to the adventure of the man with the twisted lip. Well, I have no doubt that this small matter will fall into the same innocent category. You know Peterson, the commissioner?"

"Yes."

"It is to him that this trophy belongs."

"It is his hat."

"No, no, he found it. Its owner is unknown. I beg that you will look upon it not as a battered billycock, but as an intellectual problem. And, first, as to how it came here. It arrived upon Christmas morning, in company with a good fat goose, which is, I have no doubt, roasting at this moment in front of Peterson's fire. The facts are these: about four o'clock on Christmas morning, Peterson, who, as you know, is a very honest fellow, was returning from some small jollification and was making his way homeward down Tottenham Court Road. In front of him he saw, in the gaslight, a tallish man, walking with a slight stagger, and carrying a white goose slung over his shoulder. As he reached the corner of Goodge Street, a row broke out between this stranger and a little knot of roughs. One of the latter knocked off the man's hat, on which he raised his stick to defend himself and, swinging it over his head, smashed the shop window behind him. Peterson had rushed forward to protect the stranger from his assailants; but the man, shocked at having broken the window, and seeing an official-looking person in uniform rushing towards him, dropped his goose, took to his heels, and vanished amid the labyrinth of small streets which lie at the back of Tottenham Court Road. The roughs had also fled at the appearance of Peterson, so that he was left in possession of the field of battle, and also of the spoils of victory in the shape of this battered hat and a most unimpeachable Christmas goose."

"Which surely he restored to their owner?"

"My dear fellow, there lies the problem. It is true that *For Mrs. Henry Baker* was printed upon a small card which was tied to the bird's left leg, and it is also true that the initials *H. B.* are legible upon the lining of this hat. But as there are some thousands of Bakers, and some hundreds of Henry Bakers in this city of ours, it is not easy to restore lost property to any one of them."

"What, then, did Peterson do?"

"He brought round both hat and goose to me on Christmas morning, knowing that even the smallest problems are of interest to me. The goose we retained until this morning, when there were signs that, in spite of the slight frost, it would be well that it should be eaten without unnecessary delay. Its finder has carried it off, therefore, to fulfil the ultimate destiny of a goose, while I continue to retain the hat of the unknown gentleman who lost his Christmas dinner."

"Did he not advertise?"

"No."

"Then, what clue could you have as to his identity?"

"Only as much as we can deduce."

"From his hat?"

"Precisely."

"But you are joking. What can you gather from this old battered felt?"

"Here is my lens. You know my methods. What can you gather yourself as to the individuality of the man who has worn this article?"

I took the tattered object in my hands and turned it over rather ruefully. It was a very ordinary black hat of the usual round shape—hard and much the worse for wear. The lining had been of red silk, but was a good deal discolored. There was no maker's name; but, as Holmes had remarked, the initials *H. B.* were scrawled upon one side. It was pierced in the brim for a hat-securer, but the elastic was missing. For the rest, it was cracked, exceedingly dusty, and spotted in several places, although there seemed to have been some attempt to hide the discolored patches by smearing them with ink.

"I can see nothing," said I, handing it back to my friend.

"On the contrary, Watson, you can see everything. You fail, however, to reason from what you see. You are too timid in drawing your inferences."

"Then, pray tell me what it is that you can infer from this hat?"

He picked it up and gazed at it in the peculiar introspective fashion which was characteristic of him. "It is perhaps less suggestive than it might have been," he remarked, "and yet there are a few inferences which are very distinct, and a few others which represent at least a strong balance of probability. That the man was highly intellectual is of course obvious upon the face of it, and also that he was fairly well to do within the last three years, although he has now fallen upon evil days. He had foresight, but has less now than formerly, pointing to a moral retrogression, which, when taken with the decline of his fortunes, seems to indicate some evil influence, probably drink, at work upon him. This may account also for the obvious fact that his wife has ceased to love him."

"My dear Holmes!"

"He has, however, retained some degree of self-respect," he continued, disregarding my remonstrance. "He is a man who leads a sedentary life, goes out little, is out of training entirely, is middle-aged, has grizzled hair which he has had cut within the last few days, and which he anoints with hair cream. These are the more patent facts which are to be deduced from his hat. Also, by the way, that it is extremely improbable that he has gas turned on in his house."

"You are certainly joking, Holmes."

"Not in the least. Is it possible that even now, when I give you these results, you are unable to see how they are attained?"

"I have no doubt that I am very stupid, but I must confess that I am unable to follow you. For example, how did you deduce that this man was intellectual?"

For answer Holmes clapped the hat upon his head. It came right over the forehead and settled upon the bridge of his nose. "It is a question of cubic capacity," said he; "a man with so large a brain must have something in it."

"The decline of his fortunes, then?"

"This hat is three years old. These flat brims curled at the edge came in then. It is a hat of the very best quality. Look at the band of ribbed silk and the excellent lining. If this man could afford to buy so expensive a hat three years ago, and has had no hat since, then he has assuredly gone down in the world."

"Well, that is clear enough, certainly. But how about the foresight and the moral retrogression?"

Sherlock Holmes laughed. "Here is the foresight," said he, putting his finger upon the little disc and loop of the hat-securer. "They are never sold upon hats. If this man ordered one, it is a sign of a certain amount of foresight, since he went out of his way to take this precaution against the wind. But since we see that he has broken the elastic and has not troubled to replace it, it is obvious that he has less foresight now than formerly, which is a distinct proof of a weakening nature. On the other hand, he has endeavored to conceal some of these stains upon the felt by daubing them with ink, which is a sign that he has not entirely lost his self-respect."

"Your reasoning is certainly plausible."

"The further points, that he is middle-aged, that his hair is grizzled, that it has been recently cut, and that he uses hair cream, are all to be gathered from a close examination of the lower part of the lining. The lens discloses a large number of hair-ends, clean cut by the scissors of the barber. They all appear to be adhesive, and there is a distinct odor of hair cream. This dust, you will observe, is not the gritty, gray dust of the street but the fluffy brown dust of the house, showing that it has been hung up indoors most of the time, while the marks of moisture upon the inside are proof positive that the wearer perspired very freely, and could therefore, hardly be in the best of condition."

"But his wife—you said that she had ceased to love him."

"This hat has not been brushed for weeks. When I see you, my dear Watson, with a week's accumulation of dust upon your hat, and when your wife allows you to go out in such a state, I shall fear that you also have been unfortunate enough to lose your wife's affection."

"But he might be a bachelor."

"Nay, he was bringing home the goose as a peace-offering to his wife. Remember the card upon the bird's leg."

"You have an answer to everything. But how on earth do you deduce that the gas is not turned on in his house?"

"One tallow stain, or even two, might come by chance; but when I see no less than five, I think that there can be little doubt that the individual must be brought into frequent contact with burning tallow—walks upstairs at night probably with his hat in one hand and a guttering candle in the other. Anyhow, he never got tallow-stains from a gas jet. Are you satisfied?"

"Well, it is very ingenious," said I, laughing; "but since, as you said just now, there has been no crime committed, and no harm done save the loss of a goose, all this seems to be rather a waste of energy."

The Adventure of the Blue Carbuncle

Sherlock Holmes had opened his mouth to reply, when the door flew open, and Peterson, the commissioner, rushed into the apartment with flushed cheeks and the face of a man who is dazed with astonishment.

"The goose, Mr. Holmes! The goose, sir!" he gasped.

"Eh? What of it, then? Has it returned to life and flapped off through the kitchen window?" Holmes twisted himself round upon the sofa to get a fairer view of the man's excited face.

"See here, sir! See what my wife found in its crop!" He held out his hand and displayed upon the center of the palm a brilliantly scintillating blue stone, smaller than a bean in size, but of such purity and radiance that it twinkled like an electric point in the dark hollow of his hand.

Sherlock Holmes sat up with a whistle. "My word, Peterson!" said he, "this is treasure trove indeed. I suppose you know what you have got?"

"A diamond, sir? A precious stone. It cuts into glass as though it were putty."

"It's more than a precious stone. It is the precious stone."

"Not the Countess of Morcar's blue carbuncle!" I exclaimed.

"Precisely so. I ought to know its size and shape, seeing that I have read the advertisement about it in the *Times* every day lately. It is absolutely unique, and its value can only be conjectured, but the reward offered of one thousand pounds is certainly not within a twentieth part of the market price."

"A thousand pounds!" The commissioner plumped down into a chair and stared from one to the other of us.

"That is the reward, and I have reason to know that there are sentimental considerations in the background which would induce the Countess to part with half her fortune if she could but recover the gem."

"It was lost, if I remember aright, at the Hotel Cosmopolitan," I remarked.

"Precisely so," said Holmes, "on December twenty-second, just five days ago. John Horner, a plumber, was accused of having abstracted it from the lady's jewel case. The evidence against him was so strong that the case has been referred to the courts. I have some account of the matter here, I believe." He rummaged amid his newspapers, glancing over the dates, until at last he smoothed one out, doubled it over, and read the following paragraphs:

> **Hotel Cosmopolitan Jewel Robbery.** John Horner, 26, plumber, was brought up upon the charge of having upon the 22d inst., abstracted from the jewel case of the Countess of Morcar the valuable gem known as the blue carbuncle. James Ryder, upper-attendant at the hotel, gave his evidence to the effect that he had shown Horner up to the dressing room of the Countess of Morcar upon the day of the robbery in order that he might solder the second bar of the grate, which was loose.
>
> He had remained with Horner some little time, but had finally been called away. On returning, he found that Horner had disappeared, that the bureau had been forced open, and that the small morocco casket in which, as it afterwards transpired, the Countess was accustomed to keep her jewel, was lying empty upon the dressing table. Ryder instantly gave the alarm, and Horner was arrested the same evening; but the stone could not be found either upon his person or in his rooms.
>
> Catherine Cusack, maid to the Countess, testified to having heard Ryder's cry of dismay on discovering the robbery, and to having rushed into the room, where she found matters as described by the last witness.
>
> Inspector Bradstreet, B division, gave evidence as to the arrest of Horner, who struggled frantically, and protested his innocence in the strongest terms. Evidence of a previous conviction for robbery having been given against the prisoner, the magistrate refused to deal summarily with the offence, but referred it to the courts.

Horner, who had shown signs of intense emotion during the proceedings, fainted away at the conclusion and was carried out of the hall.

"Hmm. So much for the police court," said Holmes thoughtfully, tossing aside the paper. "The question for us now to solve is the sequence of events leading from a rifled jewel case at one end to the crop of a goose in Tottenham Court Road at the other. You see, Watson, our little deductions have suddenly assumed a much more important and less innocent aspect. Here is the stone; the stone came from the goose, and the goose came from Mr. Henry Baker, the gentleman with the bad hat and all the other characteristics with which I have bored you. So now we must set ourselves very seriously to finding this gentleman and ascertaining what part he has played in this little mystery. To do this, we must try the simplest means first, and these lie undoubtedly in an advertisement in all the evening papers. If this fails, I shall have recourse to other methods."

"What will you say?"

"Give me a pencil, Peterson, and that slip of paper. Now, then: 'Found at the corner of Goodge Street, a goose and a black felt hat. Mr. Henry Baker can reclaim the same by inquiring at 6:30 this evening at 221B, Baker Street.' There. That is clear and concise."

"Very. But will he see it?"

"Well, he is sure to keep an eye on the papers, since, to a poor man, the loss was a heavy one. He was clearly so scared by his mischance in breaking the window and by the approach of Peterson that he thought of nothing but flight, but since then he must have bitterly regretted the impulse which caused him to drop his bird. Then, again, the introduction of his name will cause him to see it, for everyone who knows him will direct his attention to it. Here you are, Peterson, run down to the advertising agency and have this put in the evening papers."

"In which, sir?"

"Oh, in the *Globe, Star, Pall Mall, St. James's, Evening News Standard, Echo,* and any others that occur to you."

"Very well, sir. And this stone?"

"Ah, yes, I shall keep the stone. Thank you. And, I say, Peterson, just buy a goose on your way back and leave it here with me, for we must have one to give to this gentleman in place of the one which your family is now devouring."

When the commissioner had gone, Holmes took up the stone and held it against the light. "It's a bonny thing," said he. "Just see how it glints and sparkles. It is, of course, a nucleus and focus of crime. Every good stone is. They are the devil's pet baits. In the larger and older jewels every facet may stand for a bloody deed. This stone is not yet twenty years old. It was found in the banks of the Amoy River in southern China and is remarkable in having every characteristic of the carbuncle, save that it is blue in shade instead of ruby red. In spite of its youth, it has already a sinister history. There have been two murders, an acid throwing, a suicide, and several robberies brought about for the sake of this forty-grain weight of crystallized charcoal. Who would think that so pretty a toy would be a purveyor to the gallows and the prison? I'll lock it up in my strong box now and drop a line to the Countess to say that we have it."

"Do you think that this man Horner is innocent?"

"I cannot tell."

"Well, then, do you imagine that this other one, Henry Baker, had anything to do with the matter?"

"It is, I think, much more likely that Henry Baker is an absolutely innocent man, who had no idea that the bird which he was carrying was of considerably more value than if it were made of solid gold. That, however, I shall determine by a very simple test if we have an answer to our advertisement."

"And you can do nothing until then?"

"Nothing."

The Adventure of the Blue Carbuncle

"In that case I shall continue my professional round. But I shall come back in the evening at the hour you have mentioned, for I should like to see the solution of so tangled a business."

"Very glad to see you. I dine at seven. There is a woodcock, I believe. By the way, in view of recent occurrences, perhaps I ought to ask Mrs. Hudson to examine its crop."

I had been delayed at a case, and it was a little after half-past six when I found myself in Baker Street once more. As I approached the house I saw a tall man in a Scotch bonnet with a coat which was buttoned up to his chin waiting outside in the bright semicircle which was thrown from the fanlight. Just as I arrived the door was opened, and we were shown up together to Holmes's room.

"Mr. Henry Baker, I believe," said he, rising from his armchair and greeting his visitor with the easy air of geniality which he could so readily assume. "Pray take this chair by the fire, Mr. Baker. It is a cold night, and I observe that your circulation is more adapted for summer than for winter. Ah, Watson, you have just come at the right time. Is this your hat, Mr. Baker?"

"Yes, sir, that is undoubtedly my hat."

He was a large man with rounded shoulders, a massive head, and a broad, intelligent face, sloping down to a pointed beard of grizzled brown. A touch of red in nose and cheeks, with a slight tremor of his extended hand, recalled Holmes's surmise as to his habits. His rusty black frock coat was buttoned right up in front, with the collar turned up, and his lank wrists protruded from his sleeves without a sign of cuff or shirt. He spoke in a slow staccato fashion, choosing his words with care, and gave the impression generally of a man of learning and letters who had been ill used by the hands of fortune.

"We have retained these things for some days," said Holmes, "because we expected to see an advertisement from you giving your address. I am at a loss to know now why you did not advertise."

Our visitor gave a rather shamefaced laugh. "Shillings have not been so plentiful with me as they once were," he remarked. "I had no doubt that the gang of roughs who assaulted me had carried off both my hat and the bird. I did not care to spend more money in a hopeless attempt at recovering them."

"Very naturally. By the way, about the bird, we were compelled to eat it."

"To eat it!" Our visitor half rose from his chair in his excitement.

"Yes, it would have been of no use to anyone had we not done so. But I presume that this other goose upon the sideboard, which is about the same weight and perfectly fresh, will answer your purpose equally well?"

"Oh, certainly, certainly," answered Mr. Baker with a sigh of relief.

"Of course, we still have the feathers, legs, crop, and so on of your own bird, so if you wish—"

The man burst into a hearty laugh. "They might be useful to me as relics of my adventure," said he, "but beyond that I can hardly see what use the scattered remains of my late acquaintance are going to be to me. No, sir, I think that, with your permission, I will confine my attentions to the excellent bird which I perceive upon the sideboard."

Sherlock Holmes glanced sharply across at me with a slight shrug of his shoulders.

"There is your hat, then, and there your bird," said he. "By the way, would you tell me where you got the other one from? I am somewhat of a fowl fancier, and I have seldom seen a better grown goose."

"Certainly, sir," said Baker, who had risen and tucked his newly gained property under his arm. "There are a few of us who frequent the Alpha Inn, near the Museum—we are to be found in the Museum itself during the day, you understand. This year our good host, Windigate by name, instituted a goose club, by which, on consideration of some few pence every week, we were each to receive a bird at Christmas. My pence were duly paid, and the rest is familiar to you. I am much indebted to you, sir, for a Scotch bonnet is fitted neither to my years nor my gravity." With a comical pomposity of manner he bowed solemnly to both of us and strode off upon his way.

"So much for Mr. Henry Baker," said Holmes when he had closed the door behind him. "It is quite certain that he knows nothing whatever about the matter. Are you hungry, Watson?"

"Not particularly."

"Then I suggest that we turn our dinner into a supper and follow up this clue while it is still hot."

"By all means."

It was a bitter night, so we drew on our overcoats and wrapped cravats about our throats. Outside, the stars were shining coldly in a cloudless sky, and the breath of the passersby blew out into smoke like so many pistol shots. Our footfalls rang out crisply and loudly as we swung through the doctors' quarter, Wimpole Street, Harley Street, and so through Wigmore Street into Oxford Street. In a quarter of an hour we were in Bloomsbury at the Alpha Inn, which is a small public house at the corner of one of the streets which runs down into Holborn. Holmes pushed open the door and turned to address the ruddy-faced, white-aproned landlord.

"You have excellent geese in this establishment we are told," said he.

"My geese!" The man seemed surprised.

"Yes. I was speaking only half an hour ago to Mr. Henry Baker, who was a member of your goose club."

"Ah! yes, I see. But you see, sir, them's not our geese."

"Indeed! Whose, then?"

"Well, I got the two dozen from a salesman in Covent Garden."

"Indeed? I know some of them. Which was it?"

"Breckinridge is his name."

"Ah! I don't know him. Well, good health to you, landlord, and prosperity to your house. Good-night.

"Now for Mr. Breckinridge," he continued, buttoning up his coat as we came out into the frosty air. "Remember, Watson, that though we have so homely a thing as a goose at one end of this chain, we have at the other a man who will certainly get seven years' penal servitude unless we can establish his innocence. It is possible that our inquiry may but confirm his guilt but, in any case, we have a line of investigation which has been missed by the police, and which a singular opportunity has placed in our hands. Let us follow it out to the bitter end. Faces to the south, then, and quick march!"

We passed across Holborn, down Endell Street, and so through a zigzag of slums to Covent Garden Market. One of the largest stalls bore the name of Breckinridge upon it, and the pro-prietor, a horsy-looking man with a sharp face and trim side whiskers, was helping a boy to put up the shutters.

"Good evening. It's a cold night," said Holmes.

The salesman nodded and shot a questioning glance at my companion.

"Sold out of geese, I see," continued Holmes, pointing at the bare slabs of marble.

"Let you have five hundred tomorrow morning."

"That's no good."

"Well, there are some on the stall with the gas flare."

"Ah, but I was recommended to you."

"Who by?"

"The landlord of the Alpha."

"Oh, yes; I sent him a couple of dozen."

"Fine birds they were too. Now where did you get them from?"

The Adventure of the Blue Carbuncle

To my surprise the question provoked a burst of anger from the salesman.

"Now, then, mister," said he, with his head cocked and his arms akimbo, "what are you driving at? Let's have it straight now."

"It is straight enough. I should like to know who sold you the geese which you supplied to the Alpha."

"Well then, I shan't tell you. So now!"

"Oh, it is a matter of no importance; but I don't know why you should be so warm over such a trifle."

"Warm! You'd be as warm maybe, if you were as pestered as I am. When I pay good money for a good article there should be an end of the business; but it's 'Where are the geese?' and 'Who did you sell the geese to?' and 'What will you take for the geese?' One would think they were the only geese in the world, to hear the fuss that is made over them."

"Well, I have no connection with any other people who have been making inquiries," said Holmes carelessly. "If you won't tell us the bet is off, that is all. But I'm always ready to back my opinion on a matter of fowls, and I have a fiver on it that the bird I ate is country bred."

"Well, then, you've lost your fiver, for it's town bred," snapped the salesman.

"It's nothing of the kind."

"I say it is."

"I don't believe it."

"D'you think you know more about fowls than I, who have handled them ever since I was a nipper? I tell you, all those birds that went to the Alpha were town bred."

"You'll never persuade me to believe that."

"Will you bet then?"

"It's merely taking your money, for I know that I am right. But I'll have a sovereign on with you, just to teach you not to be obstinate."

The salesman chuckled grimly. "Bring me the books, Bill," said he.

The small boy brought round a small thin volume and a great greasy-backed one, laying them out together beneath the hanging lamp.

"Now then, Mr. Cocksure," said the salesman, "I thought that I was out of geese, but before I finish you'll find that there is still one left in my shop. You see this little book?"

"Well?"

"That's the list of the folk from whom I buy. D'you see? Well, then, here on this page are the country folk, and the numbers after their names are where their accounts are in the big ledger. Now, then! You see this other page in red ink? Well, that is a list of my town suppliers. Now, look at that third name. Just read it out to me."

"Mrs. Oakshott, 117 Brixton Road—249," read Holmes.

"Quite so. Now turn that up in the ledger."

Holmes turned to the page indicated. "Here you are, 'Mrs. Oakshott, 117 Brixton Road, egg and poultry supplier.'"

"Now, then, what's the last entry?"

" 'December twenty-second. Twenty-four geese at 7 shillings. 6 pence.' "

"Quite so. There you are. And underneath?"

" 'Sold to Mr. Windigate of the Alpha, at 12 shillings.' "

"What have you to say now?"

Sherlock Holmes looked deeply chagrined. He drew a sovereign from his pocket and threw it down upon the slab, turning away with the air of a man whose disgust is too deep for words. A few yards off he stopped under a lamppost and laughed in the hearty, noiseless fashion which was peculiar to him.

"When you see a man with whiskers of that cut and a racing stub protruding out of his pocket, you can always draw him by a bet," said he. "I daresay that if I had put a hundred pounds down in front of him, that man would not have given me such complete information as was drawn from him by the idea that he was besting me on a wager. Well, Watson, we are, I fancy, nearing the end of our quest, and the only point which remains to be determined is whether we should go on to this Mrs. Oakshott tonight, or whether we should wait until tomorrow. It is clear from what that surly fellow said that there are others besides ourselves who are anxious about the matter, and I should—"

His remarks were suddenly cut short by a loud hubbub which broke out from the stall which we had just left. Turning round we saw a little rat-faced fellow standing in the center of the circle of yellow light which was thrown by the swinging lamp, while Breckinridge, the salesman, framed in the door of his stall, was shaking his fists fiercely at the cringing figure.

"I've had enough of you and your geese," he shouted. "If you come pestering me any more with your silly talk, I'll set the dog at you. You bring Mrs. Oakshott here and I'll answer her, but what have *you* to do with it? Did I buy the geese off you?"

"No; but one of them was mine all the same," whined the little man.

"Well, then, ask Mrs. Oakshott for it."

"She told me to ask you."

"Well, you can ask the King of Prussia, for all I care. I've had enough of it. Get out!" He rushed fiercely forward, and the inquirer flitted away into the darkness.

"Ha! This may save us a visit to Brixton Road," whispered Holmes. "Come with me, and we will see what is to be made of this fellow." Striding through the scattered knots of people who lounged round the flaring stalls, my companion speedily overtook the little man and touched him upon the shoulder. He sprang round, and I could see in the gaslight that every vestige of color had been driven from his face.

"Who are you then? What do you want?" he asked in a quavering voice.

"You will excuse me," said Holmes blandly, "but I could not help overhearing the questions which you put to the salesman just now. I think that I could be of assistance to you."

"You? Who are you? How could you know anything of the matter?"

"My name is Sherlock Holmes. It is my business to know what other people don't know."

"But you can know nothing of this?"

"Excuse me, I know everything of it. You are endeavoring to trace some geese which were sold by Mrs. Oakshott of Brixton Road, to a salesman named Breckinridge, by him in turn to Mr. Windigate, of the Alpha, and by him to his club, of which Mr. Henry Baker is a member."

"Oh, sir, you are the very man whom I have longed to meet," cried the little fellow with outstretched hands and quivering fingers. "I can hardly explain to you how interested I am in this matter."

Sherlock Holmes hailed a four-wheeler which was passing. "In that case we had better discuss it in a cozy room rather than in this windswept marketplace," said he. "But pray tell me, before we go farther, who it is that I have the pleasure of assisting."

The man hesitated for an instant. "My name is John Robinson," he answered with a sidelong glance.

"No, no; the real name," said Holmes sweetly. "It is always awkward doing business with an alias."

A flush sprang to the white cheeks of the stranger. "Well then," said he, "my real name is James Ryder."

"Precisely so. Head attendant at the Hotel Cosmopolitan. Pray step into the cab, and I shall soon be able to tell you everything which you would wish to know."

The Adventure of the Blue Carbuncle

The little man stood glancing from one to the other of us with half-frightened, half-hopeful eyes, as one who is not sure whether he is on the verge of a windfall or of a catastrophe. Then he stepped into the cab, and in half an hour we were back in the sitting room at Baker Street. Nothing had been said during our drive, but the high, thin breathing of our new companion, and the claspings and unclaspings of his hands, spoke of the nervous tension within him.

"Here we are!" said Holmes cheerily as we filed into the room. "The fire looks very seasonable in this weather. You look cold, Mr. Ryder. Pray take this chair. I will just put on my slippers before we settle this little matter of yours. Now, then. You want to know what became of those geese?"

"Yes, sir."

"Or rather, I fancy, of *that* goose. It was one bird, I imagine in which you were interested—white, with a black bar across the tail."

Ryder quivered with emotion. "Oh, sir," he cried, "can you tell me where it went to?"

"It came here."

"Here?"

"Yes, and a most remarkable bird it proved. I don't wonder that you should take an interest in it. It laid an egg after it was dead—the bonniest, brightest little blue egg that ever was seen. I have it here in my museum."

Our visitor staggered to his feet and clutched the mantelpiece with his right hand. Holmes unlocked his strongbox and held up the blue carbuncle, which shone out like a star, with a cold, brilliant, many-pointed radiance. Ryder stood glaring with a drawn face, uncertain whether to claim or to disown it.

"The game's up, Ryder," said Holmes quietly. "Hold up, man, or you'll be into the fire! Give him an arm back into his chair, Watson. He's not got blood enough to go in for felony with impunity. So! Now he looks a little more human."

For a moment he had staggered and nearly fallen, but a tinge of color had returned to his cheeks, and he sat staring with frightened eyes at his accuser.

"I have almost every link in my hands, and all the proofs which I could possibly need, so there is little which you need tell me. Still, that little may as well be cleared up to make the case complete. You had heard, Ryder, of this blue stone of the Countess of Morcar's?"

"It was Catherine Cusack who told me of it," said he in a crackling voice.

"I see—her ladyship's waiting-maid. Well, the temptation of sudden wealth so easily acquired was too much for you, as it has been for better men before you; but you were not very scrupulous in the means you used. It seems to me, Ryder, that there is the making of a very pretty villain in you. You knew that this man Horner, the plumber, had been concerned in some such matter before, and that suspicion would rest the more readily upon him. What did you do then? You made some small job in my lady's room—you and your confederate Cusack—and you managed that he should be the man sent for. Then, when he had left, you rifled the jewel case, raised the alarm, and had this unfortunate man arrested. You then—"

Ryder threw himself down suddenly upon the rug and clutched at my companion's knees. "Oh, please, have mercy!" he shrieked. "Think of my father! of my mother! It would break their hearts. I never went wrong before! I never will again. I swear it. Oh, don't bring it into court! Don't!"

"Get back into your chair!" said Holmes sternly. "It is very well to cringe and crawl now, but you thought little enough of this poor Horner in court for a crime of which he knew nothing."

"I will fly, Mr. Holmes. I will leave the country, sir. Then the charge against him will break down."

"Hmm! We will talk about that. But now let us hear a true account of the next act. How came the stone into the goose, and how came the goose into the open market? Tell us the truth, for there lies your only hope of safety."

Ryder passed his tongue over his parched lips. "I will tell you it just as it happened, sir," said he. "When Horner had been arrested, it seemed to me that it would be best for me to get away with the stone at once, for I did not know at what moment the police might not take it into their heads to search me and my room. There was no place about the hotel where it would be safe. I went out, as if on some commission, and I made for my sister's house. She had married a man named Oakshott, and lived in Brixton Road, where she fattened fowls for the market. All the way there every man I met seemed to me to be a policeman or a detective; and, although it was a cold night, the sweat was pouring down my face before I came to the Brixton Road. My sister asked me what was the matter, and why I was so pale; but I told her that I had been upset by the jewel robbery at the hotel. Then I went into the back yard and wondered what it would be best to do.

"I had a friend once called Maudsley, who went to the bad, and has just been serving his time in Pentonville. One day he had met me, and fell into talk about the ways of thieves, and how they could get rid of what they stole. I knew that he would be true to me, for I knew one or two things about him; so I made up my mind to go right on to Kilburn, where he lived, and take him into my confidence. He would show me how to turn the stone into money. But how to get to him in safety? I thought of the agonies I had gone through in coming from the hotel. I might at any moment be seized and searched, and there would be the stone in my waistcoat pocket. I was leaning against the wall at the time and looking at the geese which were waddling about round my feet, and suddenly an idea came into my head which showed me how I could beat the best detective that ever lived.

"My sister had told me some weeks before that I might have the pick of her geese for a Christmas present, and I knew that she was always as good as her word. I would take my goose now, and in it I would carry my stone to Kilburn. There was a little shed in the yard, and behind this I drove one of the birds—a fine big one, white, with a barred tail. I caught it, and prying its bill open, I thrust the stone down its throat as far as my finger could reach. The bird gave a gulp, and I felt the stone pass along its gullet and down into its crop. But the creature flapped and struggled, and out came my sister to know what was the matter. As I turned to speak to her the brute broke loose and fluttered off among the others.

" 'Whatever were you doing with that bird, Jem?' says she.

" 'Well,' said I, 'you said you'd give me one for Christmas, and I was feeling which was the fattest.'

" 'Oh,' says she, 'we've set yours aside for you—Jem's bird, we call it. It's the big white one over yonder. There's twenty-six of them, which makes one for you, and one for us, and two dozen for the market.'

" 'Thank you, Maggie,' says I; 'but if it is all the same to you, I'd rather have that one I was handling just now.'

" 'The other is a good three pound heavier,' said she, 'and we fattened it expressly for you.'

" 'Never mind. I'll have the other, and I'll take it now,' said I.

" 'Oh, just as you like,' said she, a little huffed. 'Which is it you want, then?'

" 'That white one with the barred tail, right in the middle of the flock.'

" 'Oh, very well. Kill it and take it with you.'

"Well, I did what she said, Mr. Holmes, and I carried the bird all the way to Kilburn. I told my pal what I had done, for he was a man that it was easy to tell a thing like that to. He laughed until he choked, and we got a knife and opened the goose. My heart turned to water, for there was no sign of the stone, and I knew that some terrible mistake had occurred. I left the bird, rushed back to my sister's, and hurried into the back yard. There was not a bird to be seen there.

" 'Where are they all, Maggie?' I cried.

" 'Gone to the dealer's, Jem.'

" 'Which dealer's?'

" 'Breckinridge, of Covent Garden.'

" 'But was there another with a barred tail?' I asked, 'the same as the one I chose?'

" 'Yes, Jem; there were two barred-tailed ones, and I never could tell them apart.'

"Well, then, of course I saw it all, and I ran off as hard as my feet would carry me to this man Breckinridge; but he had sold the lot at once, and not one word would he tell me as to where they had gone. You heard him yourselves tonight. Well, he has always answered me like that. My sister thinks that I am going mad. Sometimes I think that I am myself. And now . . . and now I am myself a branded thief, without ever having touched the wealth for which I sold my character. Help me! Oh help me!" He burst into convulsive sobbing, with his face buried in his hands.

There was a long silence, broken only by his heavy breathing and by the measured tapping of Sherlock Holmes's fingertips upon the edge of the table. Then my friend rose and threw open the door.

"Get out!" said he.

"What, sir! Oh, bless you!"

"No more words. Get out!"

And no more words were needed. There was a rush, a clatter upon the stairs, the bang of a door, and the crisp rattle of running footfalls from the street.

"After all, Watson," said Holmes, reaching up his hand for his clay pipe, "I am not retained by the police to supply their deficiencies. If Horner were in danger it would be another thing; but this fellow will not appear against him, and the case must collapse. I suppose that I am committing a felony, but it is just possible that I am saving a soul. This fellow will not go wrong again; he is too terribly frightened. Send him to jail now, and you make him a jailbird for life. Besides, it is the season of forgiveness.

Chance has put in our way a most singular and whimsical problem, and its solution is its own reward. If you will have the goodness to touch the bell, Doctor, we will begin another investigation."

About the Author

Sir Arthur Conan Doyle (1859-1930) was born in Edinburgh, Scotland. He began writing stories for his schoolmates when he was a young boarding student in England. Later in life when his medical practice began to falter, Doyle returned to writing to supplement his income.

Doyle's Sherlock Holmes character is one of the most recognized and most imitated detectives in the mystery genre. "The Adventure of the Blue Carbuncle" was first published in The Strand in 1892.

4

The Episode of the Diamond Links

by Grant Allen

"Let us take a trip to Switzerland," said Lady Vandrift. And anyone who knows Amelia will not be surprised to learn that we did take a trip to Switzerland accordingly. Nobody can drive Sir Charles except his wife. And nobody at all can drive Amelia.

There were difficulties at the outset, because we had not reserved rooms at the hotels beforehand, and it was well on in the season; but we found ourselves in due time pleasantly quartered in Lucerne, at that most comfortable of European hostelries, the Schweitzerhof.

We were a square party of four—Sir Charles and Amelia, myself and Isabel. We had nice big rooms on the first floor overlooking the lake, and as none of us was possessed with the faintest symptom of that insane desire to climb mountain heights of disagreeable steepness and unnecessary snowiness, I will venture to assert we all enjoyed ourselves. We spent most of our time sensibly in lounging about the lake on the jolly little steamers; and when we did a mountain climb, it was on the Rigi or Pilatus where an engine undertook all the muscular work for us.

As usual, at the hotel, a great many miscellaneous people showed a burning desire to be especially nice to us. If you wish to see how friendly and charming humanity is, just try being a well-known millionaire for a week, and you'll learn a thing or two.

Wherever Sir Charles goes, he is surrounded by charming and disinterested people, all eager to make his distinguished acquaintance, and all familiar with several excellent investments or several deserving objects of Christian charity. It is my business in life, as his brother-in-law and secretary, to decline with thanks the excellent investments, and to throw judicious cold water on the objects of charity. Even I myself, as the great man's almoner, am very much sought after. People casually share with me the artless stories of "poor curates in Cumberland, you know, Mr. Wentworth," or widows in Cornwall, penniless poets with epics in their desks, and young painters who need but the breath of a patron to open to them the doors of an admiring Academy. I smile and look wise while I administer cold water in minute doses; but I never report one of these cases to Sir Charles, except in the rare or almost unheard-of event where I think there is really something in them.

Ever since our unfortunate little adventure with the Colonel at Nice, Sir Charles, who is constitutionally cautious, had been even more careful than usual about possible sharpers. And, as chance would have it, there sat just opposite us at the table at the Schweitzerhof—'tis a fad of Amelia's to dine at the hotel restaurant as she can't bear to be boxed up all day in private rooms with "too much family"—a sinister looking man with dark hair and eyes, conspicuous by his bushy, overhanging eyebrows. My attention was first called to the eyebrows in question by a nice little parson who sat at our side, and who observed that they were made up of certain large and bristly hairs. Very pleasant little fellow, this fresh-faced young parson, on his honeymoon tour with a nice wee wife, a bonnie Scotch lassie with a charming accent.

I looked at the eyebrows close. Then a sudden thought struck me. "Do you believe they're his own?" I asked of the curate. "Or are they only stuck on—a disguise? They really almost look like it."

"You don't suppose—" Charles began, and checked himself suddenly.

"Yes, I do," I answered. "The Colonel!" Then I recollected my blunder, and looked down sheepishly. For, to say the truth, Vandrift had straightly enjoined on me long before to say nothing of our painful little episode at Nice to Amelia; he was afraid if she once heard of it, he would hear of it for ever after.

"What Colonel?" the little parson inquired, with parsonical curiosity.

I noticed the man with the overhanging eyebrows give a queer sort of start. Charles's glance was fixed upon me. I hardly knew what to answer.

"Oh, a man who was at Nice with us last year," I stammered out, trying hard to look unconcerned. "A fellow they talked about, that's all." And I turned the subject.

But the curate, like a donkey, wouldn't let me turn it.

"Had he eyebrows like that?" he inquired, in an undertone. I was really angry. If this *was* Colonel Clay, the curate was obviously giving him the cue, and making it much more difficult for us to catch him now that we might possibly have lighted on the chance of doing so.

"No, he hadn't," I answered, testily. "It was a passing expression. But this is not the man. I was mistaken, no doubt." And I nudged him gently.

The little curate was too innocent for anything. "Oh, I see," he replied, nodding hard and looking wise. Then he turned to his wife, and made an obvious face, which the man with the eyebrows couldn't fail to notice.

Fortunately, a political discussion going on a few places further down the table spread up to us and diverted attention for a moment. The magical name of Gladstone saved us. Sir Charles flared up. I was truly pleased, for I could see Amelia was boiling over with curiosity by this time.

After dinner, in the billiard room, however, the man with the big eyebrows sidled up and began to talk to me. If he was Colonel Clay, it was evident he bore us no grudge at all for the five thousand pounds he had done us out of. On the contrary, he seemed quite prepared to do us out of five thousand more when opportunity offered; for he introduced himself at once as Dr. Hector MacPherson, the exclusive grantee of extensive concessions from the Brazilian Government on the Upper Amazons. He dived into conversation with me at once as to the splendid mineral resources of his Brazilian estate—the silver, the platinum, the actual rubies, the possible diamonds. I listened and smiled; I knew what was coming. All he needed to develop this magnificent concession was a little more capital. It was sad to see thousands of pounds' worth of platinum and carloads of rubies just crumbling in the soil or carried away by the river, for want of a few hundreds to work them with properly. If he knew of anybody, now, with money to invest, he could recommend him—nay, offer him—a unique opportunity of earning, say . . . forty percent on his capital, on unimpeachable security.

"I wouldn't do it for every man," Dr. Hector MacPherson remarked, drawing himself up, "but if I took a fancy to a fellow who had command of ready cash, I might choose to put him in the way of feathering his nest with unexampled rapidity."

"Exceedingly kind of you," I answered, dryly, fixing my eyes on his eyebrows.

The little curate, meanwhile, was playing billiards with Sir Charles. His glance followed mine as it rested for a moment on the bristly hairs.

"False, obviously false," he remarked with his lips, and I'm bound to confess I never saw any man speak so well by movement alone. You could follow every word, though not a sound escaped him.

During the rest of that evening, Dr. Hector MacPherson stuck to me as close as a mustard plaster. And he was almost as irritating. I got heartily sick of the Upper Amazons. I have positively waded in my time through ruby mines—in prospectuses, I mean—till the mere sight of a ruby absolutely sickens me. By the time I went to bed I was prepared to sink the Upper Amazons in the sea, and to stab, shoot, poison, or otherwise seriously damage the man with the concession and the false eyebrows.

For the next three days, at intervals, he returned to the charge. He bored me to death with his platinum and his rubies. He didn't want a capitalist who would personally exploit the thing; he would prefer to do it all on his own account, giving the capitalist a voucher from his bogus company and a lien on the concession.

I listened and smiled; I listened and yawned; I listened and was rude; I ceased to listen at all; but still, he droned on with it. I fell asleep on the steamer one day, and woke up in ten minutes to hear him droning yet: "And the yield of platinum per ton was certified to be . . ." I forget how many pounds, or ounces, or pennyweights. These details of assays have ceased to interest me; I have seen too many of them.

The fresh-faced little curate and his wife however, were quite different people. He was a cricketing Oxford man; she was a breezy Scotch lass, with a wholesome breath of the Highlands about her. I called her "White Heather." Their name was Brabazon. Millionaires are so accustomed to being beset by harpies of every description, that when they come across a young couple who are simple and natural, they delight in the purely human relation. We picnicked and went on excursions with the honeymooners. They were so frank in their young love, and so proof against chaff, that we all really liked them. But whenever I called the pretty girl "White Heather," she looked so shocked, and cried, "Oh, Mr. Wentworth!" Still, we were the best of friends. The curate offered to row us in a boat on the lake one day, while the Scotch lassie assured us she could take an oar almost as well as he did. However, we did not accept their offer, as rowboats exert an unfavorable influence upon Amelia's digestive organs.

"Nice young fellow, that man Brabazon," Sir Charles said to me one day, as we lounged together along the quay. "Never talks about advancement. Doesn't seem to me to care two pins about promotion. Says he's quite content in his country parish; enough to live upon, and needs no more; and his wife has a little, a very little, money. I asked him about his poor today, on purpose to test him. These parsons are always trying to squeeze something out of one for their poor; men in my position know the truth of the saying that we have that class of the population always with us. Would you believe it, he says he hasn't any poor at all in his parish! They're all well-to-do farmers or else able-bodied laborers, and his one terror is that somebody will come and try to pauperize them. 'If a philanthropist were to give me fifty pounds today for use at Empingham,' he said, 'I assure you, Sir Charles, I shouldn't know what to do with it. I think I should buy new dresses for Jessie, who wants them about as much as anybody else in the village—that is to say, not at all.' There's a parson for you, Seymour, my boy. Only wish we had one of his sort at Seldon."

"He certainly doesn't want to get anything out of you," I answered.

That evening at dinner, a queer little episode happened. The man with the eyebrows began talking to me across the table in his usual fashion, full of his wearisome concession on the Upper Amazons. I was trying to squash him as politely as possible, when I caught Amelia's eye. Her look amused me. She was engaged in making signals to Charles at her side to observe the little curate's curious cuff links. I glanced at them, and saw at once that they were a singular possession for so unobtrusive a person. They consisted each of a short gold bar for one arm of the link, fastened by a tiny chain of the same material to what seemed to my tolerably experienced eye, a first-rate diamond. Pretty big diamonds, too, and of remarkable shape, brilliancy, and cutting. In a moment, I knew what Amelia meant. She owned a diamond necklace, said to be of Indian origin, but short by two stones for the circumference of her tolerably ample neck.

Now, she had long been wanting two diamonds like these to match her set, but owing to the unusual shape and antiquated cutting of her own gems, she had never been able to complete the necklace, at least without removing an extravagant amount from a much larger stone.

The Episode of the Diamond Links

The Scotch lassie's eyes caught Amelia's at the same time, and she broke into a pretty smile of good-humored amusement. "You've taken in another person, Dick, dear!" she exclaimed, in her breezy way, turning to her husband. "Lady Vandrift is observing your diamond cuff links."

"They're very fine gems," Amelia observed, incautiously. (A most unwise admission, if she desired to buy them.)

But the pleasant little curate was too transparently simple a soul to take advantage of her slip of judgment. "They are good stones," he replied, "very good stones—considering. They're not diamonds at all, to tell you the truth. At best they're old-fashioned Oriental paste. My great-grandfather bought them, after the siege of Seringapatam, for a few rupees, from a Sepoy who had looted them from Tippoo Sultan's palace. He thought, like you, he had got a good thing. But it turned out, when they came to be examined by experts, they were only paste—very wonderful paste. It is supposed they had even imposed upon Tippoo himself, so fine is the imitation. But they are worth . . . well, say, fifty shillings at the utmost."

While he spoke, Charles looked at Amelia, and Amelia looked at Charles. Their eyes spoke volumes. The necklace was also supposed to have come from Tippoo's collection. Both drew at once an identical conclusion. These were two of the same stones, very likely torn apart and disengaged from the rest in the melee at the capture of the Indian palace.

"Can you take them off?" Sir Charles asked, blandly. He spoke in the tone that indicates business.

"Certainly," the little curate answered, smiling. "I'm accustomed to taking them off. They're always noticed. They've been kept in the family ever since the siege, as a sort of *valueless heirloom,* for the sake of the story, you know; and nobody ever sees them without asking, as you do, to examine them closely. They deceive even experts at first. But they're paste, all the same; unmitigated Oriental paste, for all that."

He took them both off, and handed them to Charles. No man in England is a finer judge of gems than my brother-in-law. I watched him narrowly. He examined them close, first with the naked eye, then with the little pocket-lens, which he always carries. "Admirable imitation," he muttered, passing them on to Amelia. "I'm not surprised they should dupe inexperienced observers."

But from the tone in which he said it, I could see at once he had satisfied himself they were real gems of unusual value. I know Charles's way of doing business so well. His glance to Amelia meant, "These are the very stones you have so long been in search of."

The Scotch lassie laughed a merry laugh. "He sees through them now, Dick," she cried. "I felt sure Sir Charles would be a judge of diamonds."

Amelia turned them over. I know Amelia too; and I knew from the way Amelia looked at them that she meant to have them. And when Amelia means to have anything, people who stand in the way may just as well spare themselves the trouble of opposing her.

They were beautiful diamonds. We found out afterwards the little curate's account was quite correct. These stones had come from the same necklace as Amelia's strand, made for a favorite wife of Tippoo's, who had presumably as expansive personal charms as our beloved sister-in-law's. More perfect diamonds have seldom been seen. They have excited the universal admiration of thieves and connoisseurs. Amelia told me afterwards that, according to legend, a Sepoy stole the necklace at the sack of the palace, and then fought with another for it. It was believed that two stones got spilt in the scuffle, and were picked up and sold by a third person, an onlooker, who had no idea of the value of his booty. Amelia had been hunting for them for several years, to complete her necklace.

"They are excellent paste," Sir Charles observed, handing them back. "It takes a first-rate judge to detect them from the reality. Lady Vandrift has a necklace much the same in character, but composed of genuine stones; and as these are so much like them, they would complete her set, to all outer appearances. I wouldn't mind giving you, say . . . ten pounds for the pair of them."

Mrs. Brabazon looked delighted. "Oh, sell them to him, Dick," she cried, "and buy me a brooch with the money! A pair of common links would do for you just as well. Ten pounds for two paste stones! It's quite a lot of money."

She said it so sweetly, with her pretty Scotch accent that I couldn't imagine how Dick had the heart to refuse her. But he did, all the same.

"No, Jess, darling," he answered. "They're worthless, I know; but they have for me a certain sentimental value, as I've often told you. My dear mother wore them, while she lived, as earrings; and as soon as she died, I had them set as links in order that I might always keep them about me. Besides, they have historical and family interest. Even a *worthless* heirloom, after all, *is* an heirloom."

Dr. Hector MacPherson looked across and intervened. "There is a part of my concession," he said, "where we have reason to believe a perfect new diamond will soon be discovered. If at any time you would care, Sir Charles, to look at my stones—when I get them—it would afford me the greatest pleasure in life to submit them to your consideration."

Sir Charles could stand it no longer. "Sir," he said, gazing across at him with his sternest air, "if your concession were as full of diamonds as Sindbad the Sailor's alley, I would not care to turn my head to look at them. I am acquainted with the nature and practice of salting." And he glared at the man with the overhanging eyebrows as if he would devour him raw.

Poor Dr. Hector MacPherson subsided instantly. We learned a little later that he was a harmless lunatic who went about the world with successive concessions for ruby mines and platinum reefs because he had been ruined and driven mad by speculations in the two, and now recouped himself by imaginary grants in Burmah and Brazil, or anywhere else that turned up handy. And his eyebrows, after all, were of nature's handicraft. We were sorry for the incident; but a man in Sir Charles's position is such a mark for rogues that, if he did not take means to protect himself promptly, he would be for ever overrun by them.

When we went up to our room that evening, Amelia flung herself on the sofa. "Charles," she broke out in the voice of a tragedy queen, "those are real diamonds, and I shall never be happy again till I get them."

"They are real diamonds," Charles echoed. "And you shall have them, Amelia. They're worth not less than three thousand pounds. But I shall bid them up gently."

So, next day, Charles set to work to haggle with the curate. Brabazon, however, didn't care to part with them. He was no moneygrubber, he said. He cared more for his mother's gift and a family tradition than for a hundred pounds, if Sir Charles were to offer it. Charles's eye gleamed. "But if I give you *two* hundred!" he said, insinuatingly. "What opportunities for good! You could build a new wing to your village school-house!"

"We have ample accommodation," the curate answered. "No, I don't think I'll sell them."

Still, his voice faltered somewhat, and he looked down at them inquiringly.

Charles was too quick. "A hundred pounds more or less matters little to me," he said, "and my wife has set her heart on them. It's every man's duty to please his wife—isn't it, Mrs. Brabazon? I offer you three hundred."

The little Scotch girl clasped her hands. "Three hundred pounds! Oh, Dick, just think what fun we could have, and what good we could do with it! Do let him have them."

Her accent was irresistible. But the curate shook his head. "Impossible," he answered. "My dear mother's earrings! Uncle Aubrey would be so angry if he knew I'd sold them. I daren't face Uncle Aubrey."

"Has he expectations from Uncle Aubrey?" Sir Charles asked of White Heather.

Mrs. Brabazon laughed. "Uncle Aubrey! Oh, dear, no. Poor dear old Uncle Aubrey! Why, the darling old soul hasn't a penny to bless himself with, except his pension. He's a retired post captain." And she laughed melodiously. She was a charming woman.

"Then I should disregard Uncle Aubrey's feelings," Sir Charles said, decisively.

"No, no," the curate answered. "Poor dear old Uncle Aubrey. I wouldn't do anything for the world to annoy him. And he'd be sure to notice it."

We went back to Amelia. "Well, have you got them?" she asked.

"No," Sir Charles answered. "Not yet. But he's coming round, I think. He's hesitating now. Would rather like to sell them himself, but is afraid of what 'Uncle Aubrey' would say about the matter. His wife will talk him out of his needless consideration for Uncle Aubrey's feelings, and tomorrow we'll finally clench the bargain."

Next morning we stayed late in our salon, where we always breakfasted, and did not come down to the public rooms till just before noon, Sir Charles being busy with me over tardy correspondence. When we did come down, the concierge stepped forward with a twisted little feminine note for Amelia. She took it and read it. Her countenance fell. "There, Charles," she cried, handing it to him, "you've let the chance slip. I shall never be happy now! They've gone off with the diamonds."

Charles seized the note and read it. Then he passed it on to me. It was short, but final:

Thursday, 6 a.m.

Dear Lady Vandrift,

Will you kindly excuse our having gone off hurriedly without bidding you good-bye? We have just had a horrid telegram to say that Dick's favorite sister is dangerously ill of fever in Paris. I wanted to shake hands with you before we left—you have all been so sweet to us—but we go by the morning train, absurdly early, and I wouldn't for all the world disturb you.

Perhaps some day we may meet again, though, buried as we are in a North-country village, it isn't likely. But in any case, you have secured the grateful recollection of yours very cordially,

Jessie Brabazon.

p.s. Kindest regards to Sir Charles and those dear Wentworths, and a kiss for yourself, if I may venture to send you one.

"She doesn't even mention where they've gone," Amelia exclaimed, in a very bad humor.

"The concierge may know," Isabel suggested, looking over my shoulder.

We asked at his office.

Yes, the gentleman's address was the Rev. Richard Peploe Brabazon, Holme Bush Cottage, Empingham, Northumberland.

Any address where letters might be sent at once, in Paris?

For the next ten days, or till further notice, Hotel des Deux Mondes, Avenue de l'Opera.

Amelia's mind was made up at once. "Strike while the iron's hot," she cried. "This sudden illness, coming at the end of their honeymoon, and involving ten days' more stay at an expensive hotel, will probably upset the curate's budget. He'll be glad to sell now. You'll get them for three hundred. It was absurd of Charles to offer so much at first, but offered once, of course we must stick to it."

"What do you propose to do?" Charles asked. "Write, or telegraph?"

"Oh, how silly men are!" Amelia cried. "Is this the sort of business to be arranged by letter, still less by telegram? No. Seymour must start off at once, taking the night train to Paris; and the moment he gets there, he must interview the curate or Mrs.

The Episode of the Diamond Links

Brabazon. Mrs. Brabazon's the best. She has none of this stupid, sentimental nonsense about Uncle Aubrey."

It is not part of a secretary's duties to act as a diamond broker. But when Amelia puts her foot down, she puts her foot down—a fact which she is unnecessarily fond of emphasizing in that identical proposition. So the selfsame evening saw me safe in the train on my way to Paris; and next morning I turned out of my comfortable sleeping car at the Gare de Strasbourg. My orders were to bring back those diamonds, dead or alive so to speak, in my pocket, to Lucerne; and to offer any needful sum, up to two thousand five hundred pounds, for their immediate purchase.

When I arrived at the Deux Mondes I found the poor little curate and his wife both greatly agitated. They had sat up all night, they said, with their invalid sister and the sleeplessness and suspense had certainly told upon them after their long railway journey. They were pale and tired, Mrs. Brabazon in particular looking ill and worried—too much like White Heather. I was more than half-ashamed of bothering them about the diamonds at such a moment, but it occurred to me that Amelia was probably right. They would now have reached the end of the sum set apart for their Continental trip; and a little ready cash might be far from unwelcome.

I broached the subject delicately. It was a fad of Lady Vandrift's, I said. She had set her heart upon those useless trinkets. And she wouldn't go without them. She must and would have them. But the curate was obdurate. He threw Uncle Aubrey still in my teeth. Three hundred?—no, never! A mother's present; impossible, dear Jessie! Jessie begged and prayed; she had grown really attached to Lady Vandrift, she said; but the curate wouldn't hear of it. I went up tentatively to four hundred. He shook his head gloomily. It wasn't a question of money, he said. It was a question of affection. I saw it was no use trying that tack any longer.

I struck out a new line. "These stones," I said, "I think I ought to inform you, are really diamonds. Sir Charles is certain of it. Now, is it right for a man of your profession and position to be wearing a pair of big gems like those, worth several hundred pounds, as ordinary cuff links? A woman? Yes, I grant you; but for a man, is it manly? And you a cricketer!"

He looked at me and laughed. "Will nothing convince you?" he cried. "They have been examined and tested by half a dozen jewelers, and we know them to be paste. It wouldn't be right of me to sell them to you under false pretenses, however unwilling on my side. I couldn't do it."

"Well, then," I said, going up a bit in my bids to meet him, "I'll put it like this. These gems are paste. But Lady Vandrift has an unconquerable and unaccountable desire to possess them. Money doesn't matter to her. She is a friend of your wife's. As a personal favor, won't you sell them to her for a thousand?"

He shook his head. "It would be wrong," he said. "I might even add, criminal."

"But we will take all the risk," I cried.

He was absolute adamant. "As a clergyman," he answered, "I feel I cannot do it."

"Will you try, Mrs. Brabazon?" I asked.

The pretty little Scotchwoman leant over and whispered. She coaxed and cajoled him. Her ways were winsome. I couldn't hear what she said, but he seemed to give way at last. "I should love Lady Vandrift to have them," she murmured, turning to me. "She is such a dear!" And she took out the links from her husband's cuffs and handed them across to me.

"How much?" I asked.

"Two thousand?" she answered interrogatively. It was a big rise all at once; but such are the ways of women.

"Done!" I replied. "Do you consent?"

The curate looked up as if ashamed of himself.

"I consent," he said, slowly, "since Jessie wishes it. But as a clergyman, and to prevent any future misunderstanding, I should like you to give me a statement in writing that you buy them on my distinct and positive declaration that they are made of paste—old Oriental paste—not genuine stones, and that I do not claim any other qualities for them."

I popped the gems into my purse, well pleased.

"Certainly," I said, pulling out a paper. Charles, with his unerring business instinct, had anticipated the request, and given me a signed agreement to that effect.

"You will take a check?" I inquired.

He hesitated.

"Notes of the Bank of France would suit me better," he answered.

"Very well," I replied. "I will go out and get them."

How very unsuspicious some people are! He allowed me go off—with the stones in my pocket!

Sir Charles had given me a blank check, not exceeding two thousand five hundred pounds. I took it to our agents and cashed it for notes of the Bank of France. The curate clasped them with pleasure. And right glad I was to go back to Lucerne that night, feeling that I had got those diamonds into my hands for about a thousand pounds under their real value.

At Lucerne railway station Amelia met me, and she was positively agitated. "Have you bought them, Seymour?" she asked.

"Yes," I answered, producing my spoils in triumph.

"Oh, how dreadful!" she cried, drawing back. "Do you think they're real? Are you sure he hasn't cheated you?"

"Certain of it," I replied, examining them. "No one can take me in, not in the matter of diamonds. Why on earth should you doubt them?"

"Because I've been talking to Mrs. O'Hagan at the hotel, and she says there's a well-known trick just like that. She's read of it in a book. A swindler has two sets, one real, one false; and he makes you buy the false ones by showing you the real, and pretending he sells them as a special favor."

"You needn't be alarmed," I answered. "I am a judge of diamonds."

"I shan't be satisfied," Amelia murmured, "till Charles has seen them."

We went up to the hotel. For the first time in her life I saw Amelia really nervous as I handed the stones to Charles to examine. Her doubt was contagious. I half feared, myself, he might break out into a deep monosyllabic interjection, losing his temper in haste, as he often does when things go wrong. But he looked at them with a smile, while I told him the price.

"Eight hundred pounds less than their value," he answered, well satisfied.

"You have no doubt of their reality?" I asked.

"Not the slightest," he replied, gazing at them. "They are genuine stones, precisely the same in quality and type as Amelia's necklace."

Amelia drew a sigh of relief. "I'll go upstairs," she said, slowly, "and bring down my own for you both to compare with them."

One minute later, she rushed down again, breathless. Amelia is far from slim, and I never before knew her exert herself so actively.

"Charles, Charles!" she cried, "Do you know what dreadful thing has happened? Two of my own stones are gone. He's stolen a couple of diamonds from my necklace, and sold them back to me."

She held out the strand. It was all too true. Two gems were missing—and these two just fitted the empty places!

A light broke in upon me. I clapped my hand to my head. "Mercy," I exclaimed, "the little curate is . . . Colonel Clay!"

Charles clapped his own hand to his brow in turn. "And Jessie," he cried, "White Heather, that innocent little Scotchwoman! I often detected a familiar ring in her voice, in spite of the charming Highland accent. Jessie is . . . Madame Picardet!"

The Episode of the Diamond Links

We had absolutely no evidence; but we felt instinctively sure of it.

Sir Charles was determined to catch the rogue. This second deception put him on his mettle. "The worst of the man is," he said, "that he has a method. He doesn't go out of his way to cheat us; he makes us go out of ours to be cheated. He lays a trap, and we tumble headlong into it. Tomorrow, Seymour, we must follow him on to Paris."

Amelia explained to him what Mrs. O'Hagan had said. Charles took it all in at once, with his usual sagacity. "That explains," he said, "why the rascal used this particular trick to draw us on by. If we had suspected him, he could have shown the diamonds were real, and so escaped detection. It was a blind to draw us off from the fact of the robbery. He went to Paris to be out of the way when the discovery was made, and to get a clear day's start of us. What a consummate rogue! And to do me twice running!"

"How did he get at my jewel case though?" Amelia exclaimed.

"That's the question," Charles answered. "You do leave it about so!"

"And why didn't he steal the whole necklace at once, and sell the gems?" I inquired.

"Too cunning," Charles replied. "This was much better business. It isn't easy to dispose of a big thing like that. In the first place, the stones are large and valuable; in the second place, they're well known. Every dealer has heard of the Vandrift necklace, and seen pictures of the shape of them. They're marked gems, so to speak. No, he played a better game—took a couple of them off, and offered them to the one person on earth who was likely to buy them without suspicion. He came here, meaning to work this very trick; he had the links made right to the shape beforehand, and then he stole the stones and slipped them into their places. It's a wonderfully clever trick. Upon my soul, I *almost* admire the fellow."

For Charles is a business man himself, and can appreciate business capacity in others.

How Colonel Clay came to know about that necklace, and to appropriate two of the stones, we only discovered much later. I will not here anticipate that disclosure. One thing at a time is a good rule in life. For the moment, he succeeded in baffling us altogether.

However, we followed him on to Paris, telegraphing beforehand to the Bank of France to stop the notes. It was all in vain. They had been cashed within half an hour of my paying them. The curate and his wife, we found, had left the Hotel des Deux Mondes for parts unknown that same afternoon. And, as usual with Colonel Clay, they vanished into space, leaving no clue behind them. In other words, they changed their disguise, no doubt, and reappeared somewhere else that night in altered characters. At any rate, no such person as the Reverend Richard Peploe Brabazon was ever afterwards heard of . . . and, for that matter, no such village exists as Empingham, Northumberland.

We communicated the matter to the Parisian police. They were most unsympathetic. "It is no doubt Colonel Clay," said the official whom we saw, "but you seem to have little just ground of complaint against him. As far as I can see, messieurs, there is not much to choose between you. You, Monsieur le Chevalier, desired to buy diamonds at the price of paste. You, madame, feared you had bought paste at the price of diamonds. You, monsieur the secretary, tried to get the stones from an unsuspecting person for half their value. He took you all in, that brave Colonel. It was diamond cut diamond."

Which was true, no doubt, but by no means consoling.

We returned to the Grand Hotel. Charles was fuming with indignation. "This is really too much," he exclaimed. "What an audacious rascal! But he will never again take me in, my dear Seymour. I only hope he'll try it. I should love to catch him. I'd know him another time, I'm sure, in spite of his disguises. It's absurd my being tricked twice running like this. But never again while I live! Never again, I declare to you!"

A courier in the hall close by murmured a response. We stood under the veranda of the Grand Hotel in the big glass courtyard, and I truly believed that courier was Colonel Clay himself in one of his disguises.

But perhaps we were beginning to suspect him everywhere.

About the Author

Charles Grant Blairfindie Allen (1848-1899) was born in Ontario, Canada. He studied philosophy and science in England, then taught briefly before starting a career as a writer. While his early works were primarily technical and scientific, he was far more successful in the field of fiction.

"The Episode of the Diamond Links" was first published in July 1896 in The Strand *and later in* An African Millionaire, *a collection of twelve stories dealing with crimes committed by the mysterious Colonel Clay.*

5

The Mystery of the
Five Hundred Diamonds

by Robert Barr

Chapter I. The Finding of the Fated Five Hundred

When I say I am called Valmont, the name will convey no impression to the reader one way or another. My occupation is that of private detective in London, but if you ask any policeman in Paris who Valmont was he will likely be able to tell you, unless he is a recent recruit. If you ask him where Valmont is now, he may not know, yet I have a good deal to do with the Parisian police.

For a period of seven years I was chief detective to the government of France, and if I am unable to prove myself a great crime hunter, it is because the record of my career is in the secret archives of Paris.

I may admit at the outset that I have no grievances to air. The French government considered itself justified in dismissing me, and did so. In this action it was quite within its right, and I should be the last to dispute that right; but on the other hand, I consider myself justified in publishing the following account of what actually occurred, especially as so many false rumors have been put abroad concerning the case. However, as I said at the beginning, I hold no grievance, because my worldly affairs are now much more prosperous than they were in Paris. My intimate knowledge of that city and the country of which it is the capital is bringing to me many cases with which I have dealt more or less successfully since I established myself in London.

Without further preliminary I shall at once plunge into an account of the case which riveted the attention of the whole world a little more than a decade ago.

The year 1893 was a prosperous twelve months for France. The weather was good, the harvest excellent, and the wine of that vintage is celebrated to this day. Everyone was well off and reasonably happy, a marked contrast to the state of things a few years later, when dissension over the Dreyfus case rent the country in twain.

Newspaper readers may remember that in 1893 the government of France fell heir to an unexpected treasure which set the civilized world agog, especially those inhabitants of it who are interested in historical relics. This was the finding of the diamond necklace in the Chateau de Chaumont, where it had rested undiscovered for a century in a rubbish heap of an attic. I believe it has not been questioned that this was the veritable necklace which the court jeweler, Boehmer, hoped to sell to Marie Antoinette, although how it came to be in the Chateau de Chaumont no one has been able to form even a conjecture.

For a hundred years it was supposed that the necklace had been broken up in London, and its half-a-thousand stones, great and small, sold separately. It has always seemed strange to me that the Countess de Lamotte-Valois, who was thought to have profited by the sale of these jewels, should not have abandoned France if she possessed money to leave that country, for exposure was inevitable if she remained. Indeed, the unfortunate woman was branded and imprisoned, and afterwards was dashed to death from the third story of a London house, when, in the direst poverty, she sought escape from the consequences of the debts she had incurred.

I am not superstitious in the least, yet this celebrated piece of treasure-trove seems actually to have exerted a malign influence over everyone who had the misfortune to be connected with it. Indeed, in a small way, I who write these words suffered dismissal and disgrace, though I caught but one glimpse of this dazzling scintillation of jewels. The jeweler who made the necklace met financial ruin. The queen for whom it was constructed was beheaded. That highborn Prince Louis Rene Edouard, Cardinal de Rohan, who purchased it, was flung into prison. The unfortunate countess, who said she acted as go-between until the transfer was concluded, clung for five awful minutes to a London windowsill before dropping to her death on the flagstones below. And now, a hundred and eight years later, up comes this devil's display of fireworks to the light again!

Droulliard, the workingman who found the ancient box, seems to have pried it open, and ignorant though he was—he had probably never seen a diamond in his life before—realized that a fortune was in his grasp. The baleful glitter from the combination must have sent madness into his brain, working havoc therein as though the shafts of brightness were those mysterious rays which scientists have recently discovered. He might quite easily have walked through the main gate of the chateau unsuspected and unquestioned with the diamonds concealed about his person. But instead of this, he crept from the attic window onto the steep roof, slipped from the eaves, and fell to the ground, while the necklace, intact, shimmered in the sunlight beside his body.

No matter where these jewels had been found the government would have insisted that they belonged to the treasury of the Republic; but as the Chateau de Chaumont was an historical monument, and the property of France, there could be no question regarding the ownership of the necklace. The government at once claimed it, and ordered it to be sent by a trustworthy military man to Paris. It was carried safely and delivered promptly to the authorities by Alfred Dreyfus, a young captain of artillery, to whom its custody had been entrusted.

In spite of its fall from the tall tower, neither case nor jewels were perceptibly damaged. The lock of the box had apparently been forced by Droulliard's hatchet, or perhaps by the clasp knife found on his body. On reaching the ground the lid had flown open, and the necklace was thrown out.

I believe there was some discussion in the cabinet regarding the fate of this ill-omened trophy, one section wishing it to be placed in a museum on account of its historical interest, another advocating the breaking up of the necklace and the selling of the diamonds for what they would fetch. But a third party maintained that the method to get the most money into the coffers of the country was to sell the necklace as it stood, for as the world now contains so many rich amateurs who collect undoubted rarities, regardless of expense, the historic associations of the jeweled collar would enhance the intrinsic value of the stones. This view prevailing, it was announced that the necklace would be sold by auction a month later in the rooms of Meyer, Renault Co., in the Boulevard des Italiens, near the Bank of the Credit-Lyonnais.

This announcement elicited much comment from the newspapers of all countries. It seemed that, from a financial point of view at least, the decision of the government had been wise, for it speedily became evident that a notable coterie of wealthy buyers would be congregated in Paris on the thirteenth when the sale was to take place. But we of the inner circle were made aware of another result somewhat more disquieting, which was that the most expert criminals in the world were also gathering like vultures upon the fair city. The honor of France was at stake. Whoever bought that necklace must be assured of a safe conduct out of the country. We might view with equanimity whatever happened afterwards, but while he was a resident of France his life and property must not be endangered. Thus it came about that I was given full authority to insure that neither murder nor theft nor both combined should be committed while the purchaser of the necklace remained within our boundaries, and for this purpose the police resources of France were placed unreservedly at my disposal. If I failed, there should be no one to blame but myself; consequently, as I have remarked before, I do not complain of my dismissal by the government.

The broken lock of the jewel case had been very deftly repaired by an expert locksmith, who in executing his task was so unfortunate as to scratch a finger on the broken metal, whereupon blood poisoning set in, and although his life was saved, he was dismissed from the hospital with his right arm gone and his usefulness destroyed.

When the jeweler Boehmer made the necklace, he asked eight hundred thousand dollars for it, but after years of disappointment he was content to sell it to Cardinal de Rohan for three hundred and twenty thousand dollars, to be liquidated in three installments, not one of which was ever paid. This latter amount was probably somewhere near the value of the five hundred and sixteen separate stones, one of which was of tremendous size, a very monarch of diamonds, holding its court among seventeen brilliants each as large as a filbert. This iridescent concentration of wealth was, as one might say, placed in my care, and I had to see to it that no harm came to the necklace or to its prospective owner until they were safely across the boundaries of France.

The four weeks previous to the thirteenth proved a busy and anxious time for me. Thousands, most of whom were actuated by mere curiosity, wished to view the diamonds. We were compelled to discriminate, and sometimes discriminated against the wrong person, which caused unpleasantness. Three distinct attempts were made to rob the safe, but luckily these criminal efforts were frustrated, and so we came unscathed to the eventful thirteenth of the month.

The sale was to begin at two o'clock, and on the morning of that day I took the somewhat tyrannical precaution of having the more dangerous of our own malefactors, and as many of the foreign thieves as I could trump up charges against, laid by the heels. Yet I knew very well it was not these rascals I had most to fear, but the suave, well-groomed gentlemen, amply supplied with unimpeachable credentials, stopping at our fine hotels and living like princes. Many of these were foreigners against whom we could prove nothing, and whose arrest might land us into temporary international difficulties. Nevertheless, I had each of them shadowed, and on the morning of the thirteenth if one of them had even disputed a cab fare I should have had him in prison half an hour later, and taken the consequences; but these gentlemen are very shrewd and do not commit mistakes.

I made up a list of all the men in the world who were able or likely to purchase the necklace. Many of them would not be present in person at the auction rooms; their bidding would be done by agents. This simplified matters a good deal, for the agents kept me duly informed of their purposes, and besides, an agent who handles treasure every week is an adept at the business, and does not need the protection which must surround an amateur, who in nine cases out of ten has but scant idea of the dangers that threaten him, beyond knowing that if he goes down a dark street in a dangerous quarter he is likely to be maltreated and robbed.

There were no less than sixteen clients all told, whom we learned were to attend personally on the day of the sale, any one of whom might well have made the purchase. The Marquis of Warlingham and Lord Oxtead from England were well-known jewel fanciers, while at least half a dozen millionaires were expected from the United States, with a smattering from Germany, Austria, and Russia, and one each from Italy, Belgium, and Holland.

Admission to the auction rooms was allowed by ticket only, to be applied for at least a week in advance, applications to be accompanied by satisfactory testimonials. It would possibly have surprised many of the rich men collected there to know that they sat cheek by jowl with some of the most noted thieves of England and America, but I allowed this for two reasons: first, I wished to keep these sharpers under my own eye until I knew who had bought the necklace; and, secondly, I was desirous that they should not know they were suspected.

I stationed trusty men outside on the Boulevard des Italiens, each of whom knew by sight most of the probable purchasers of the necklace. It was arranged that when the sale was over I should walk out to the boulevard alongside the man who was the new owner of the diamonds, and from that moment until he quitted France, my men were not to lose sight of him if he took personal custody of the stones, instead of doing the sensible and proper thing of having them insured and forwarded to his residence by some responsible transit company, or depositing them in the bank. In fact, I took every precaution that occurred to me. All of Paris was on the alert and felt itself pitted against the scoundrels of the world.

For one reason or another, it was nearly half past two before the sale began. There had been considerable delay because of forged tickets, and, indeed, each order for admittance was so closely scrutinized that this in itself took a good deal more time than we anticipated. Every chair was occupied, and still a number of the visitors were compelled to stand. I stationed myself by the swinging doors at the entrance end of the hall, where I could command a view of the entire assemblage. Some of my men were placed with backs against the wall, while others were distributed among the chairs, all in plain clothes. During the sale the diamonds themselves were not displayed, but the box containing them rested in front of the auctioneer, and three policemen in uniform stood guard on either side.

Chapter II. The Scene in the Sale Room

Very quietly the auctioneer began by saying that there was no need for him to expatiate on the noble character of the treasure he was privileged to offer for sale, and with this preliminary he requested those present to bid. Someone offered twenty thousand francs, which was received with much laughter; then the bidding went steadily on until it reached nine hundred thousand francs, which I knew to be less than half the reserve the government had placed upon the necklace. The contest advanced more slowly until the million and a half was touched, and there it hung fire for a time, while the auctioneer remarked that this sum did not equal that which the maker of the necklace had finally been forced to accept for it. After another pause he added that, as the reserve was not exceeded, the necklace would be withdrawn and probably never again offered for sale. He therefore urged those who were holding back to make their bids now. At this the contest livened until the sum of two million three hundred thousand francs had been offered, and now I knew the necklace would be sold. Nearing the three million mark the competition thinned down to a few dealers from Hamburg and the Marquis of Warlingham, from England, when a voice that had not yet been heard in the auction room was lifted in a tone of some impatience:

"One million dollars!"

There was an instant hush, followed by the scribbling of pencils, as each person present reduced the sum to its equivalent in his own currency—pounds for the English, francs for the French, marks for the German, and so on. The aggressive tone and the clear-cut face of the bidder proclaimed him an American, no less than the financial denomination he had used. In a moment it was realized that his bid was a clear leap of more than two million francs, and a sigh went up from the audience as if this settled it, and the great sale was done. Nevertheless the auctioneer's hammer hovered over the lid of his desk, and he looked up and down the long line of faces turned toward him. He seemed reluctant to tap the board, but no one ventured to compete against this tremendous sum, and with a sharp click the mallet fell.

"What name?" he asked, bending over toward the customer.

"Cash," replied the American. "Here's a check for the amount. I'll take the diamonds with me."

"Your request is somewhat unusual," protested the auctioneer mildly.

"I know what you mean," interrupted the American. "You think the check may not be cashed. You will notice it is drawn on the Credit-Lyonnais, which is practically next door. I must have the jewels with me. Send round your messenger with the check; it will take only a few minutes to find out whether or not the money is there to meet it. The necklace is mine, and I insist on having it."

The auctioneer with some demur handed the check to the representative of the French government who was present, and this official himself went to the bank. There were some other things to be sold, and the auctioneer endeavored to go on through the list, but no one paid the slightest attention to him.

Meanwhile I was studying the countenance of the man who had made the astounding bid, when I should instead have adjusted my preparations to meet the new conditions now confronting me. Here was a man about whom we knew nothing whatever. I had come to the instant conclusion that he was a prince of criminals, and that a sinister design, not at that moment fathomed by me, was afoot to get possession of the jewels. The handing up of the check was clearly a trick of some sort, and I fully expected the official to return and say the draft was good. I determined to prevent this man from getting the jewel box until I knew more of his game. Quickly I removed from my place near the door to the auctioneer's desk, having two objects in view first, to warn the auctioneer not to part with the treasure too easily; and, second, to study the suspected man at closer range. Of all evildoers, the American is most to be feared; he uses more ingenuity in the planning of his projects, and will take greater risks in carrying them out than any other malefactor on earth.

From my new station I saw there were two men to deal with. The bidder's face was keen and intellectual; his hands refined, clean, and white, showing they were long divorced from manual labor, if indeed they had ever done any useful work. Coolness and imperturbability were his beyond a doubt. The companion who sat at his right was of an entirely different stamp. His hands were hairy and suntanned; his face bore the stamp of grim determination and unflinching bravery. I knew that these two types usually hunted in couples—the one to scheme, the other to execute, and they always formed a combination dangerous to encounter and difficult to circumvent.

There was a buzz of conversation up and down the hall as these two men talked together in low tones. I knew now that I was face to face with the most hazardous problem of my life.

I whispered to the auctioneer, who bent his head to listen. He knew very well who I was, of course.

The Mystery of the Five Hundred Diamonds

"You must not give up the necklace," I began.

He shrugged his shoulders. "I am under the orders of the official from the Ministry of the Interior. You must speak to him."

"I shall not fail to do so," I replied. "Nevertheless, do not give up the box too readily."

"I am helpless," he protested with another shrug. "I obey the orders of the government."

Seeing it was useless to parley further with the auctioneer, I set my wits at work to meet the new emergency. I felt convinced that the check would prove to be genuine, and that the fraud, wherever it lay, might not be disclosed in time to aid the authorities. My duty, therefore, was to make sure we lost sight of neither the buyer nor the thing bought. Of course, I could not arrest the purchaser merely on suspicion; besides, it would make the government the laughingstock of the world if it sold a case of jewels and immediately placed the buyer in custody when the government itself had handed over his goods to him. Ridicule kills in France. A breath of laughter may blow a government out of existence in Paris much more effectually than will a whiff of cannon smoke. My duty then was to give the government full warning, and never lose sight of my man until he was clear of France; then my responsibility ended.

I took aside one of my own men in plain clothes and said to him, "You have seen the American who has bought the necklace?"

"Yes, sir."

"Very well. Go outside quietly and station yourself there. He is likely to emerge presently with the jewels in his possession. You are not to lose sight of either the man or the casket. I shall follow him and be close behind him as he emerges, and you are to shadow us. If he parts with the case you must be ready at a sign from me to follow either the man or the jewels. Do you understand?"

"Yes, sir," he answered, and left the room.

It is ever the unforeseen that baffles us; it is easy to be wise after the event. I should have sent two men, and I have often thought since how admirable is the regulation of the Italian government which sends out its policemen in pairs. Or I should have given my man power to call for help; but even as it was, he did only half as well as I had a right to expect of him, and the blunder he committed by a moment's dull-witted hesitation—ah, well! there is no use in scolding. After all the result might have been the same.

Just as my man disappeared between the two folding doors the official from the Ministry of the Interior entered. I intercepted him about halfway on his journey from the door to the auctioneer.

"Possibly the check appears to be genuine," I whispered to him.

"But certainly," he replied pompously. He was an individual greatly impressed with his own importance—the kind of character with which it is always difficult to deal. Afterwards the government asserted that this official had warned me, and the utterances of an empty-headed dolt dressed in a little brief authority, as the English poet says, were looked upon as the epitome of wisdom.

"I advise you strongly not to hand over the necklace as has been requested," I went on.

"Why?" he asked.

"Because I am convinced the bidder is a criminal."

"If you have proof of that, arrest him."

"I have no proof at the present moment, but I request you to delay the delivery of the goods."

"That is absurd," he cried impatiently. "The necklace is his, not ours. The money has already been transferred to the account of the government; we cannot retain the five million francs and refuse to hand over to him what he has bought with them," and so the man left me standing there, nonplused and anxious. The eyes of everyone in the room had been turned on us during our brief conversation, and now the official proceeded ostentatiously up the room with a grand air of importance; then, with a bow and

The Mystery of the Five Hundred Diamonds

flourish of the hand, he said dramatically, "The jewels belong to monsieur."

The two Americans rose simultaneously, the taller holding out his hand while the auctioneer passed to him the case he had apparently paid so highly for. The American nonchalantly opened the box and for the first time the electric radiance of the jewels burst upon that audience, each member of which craned his neck to behold it. It seemed to me a most reckless thing to do. He examined the jewels minutely for a few moments, then snapped the lid shut again, and calmly put the box in his outside pocket, and I could not help noticing that the light overcoat he wore possessed pockets made extraordinarily large, as if on purpose for this very case. And now this amazing man walked serenely down the room past miscreants who joyfully would have cut his throat for even the smallest diamond in that conglomeration; yet he did not take the trouble to put his hand on the pocket which contained the case, or in any way attempt to protect it. The assemblage seemed stricken dumb by his audacity. His friend followed closely at his heels, and the tall man disappeared through the folding doors. Not so the other. He turned quickly, and whipped two revolvers out of his pockets, which he presented at the astonished crowd. There had been a movement on the part of everyone to leave the room, but the sight of these deadly weapons confronting them made each one shrink into his place again.

The man with his back to the door spoke in a loud and domineering voice, asking the auctioneer to translate what he had to say into French and German; he spoke in English.

"These here shiners are valuable; they belong to my friend who has just gone out. Casting no reflections on the generality of people in this room, there are, nevertheless, half a dozen *crooks* among us whom my friend wishes to avoid. Now, no honest man here will object to giving the buyer of that there trinket five clear minutes in which to get away. It's only the *crooks* that can kick. I ask these five minutes as a favor, but if they are not granted I am going to take them as a right. Any man who moves will get shot."

"I am an honest man," I cried, "and I object. I am chief detective of the French government. Stand aside; the police will protect your friend."

"Hold on, my son," warned the American, turning one weapon directly upon me, while the other held a sort of roving commission, pointing all over the room. "My friend is from New York and he distrusts the police as much as he does the grafters. You may be twenty detectives, but if you move before that clock strikes three, I'll bring you down, and don't you forget it."

It is one thing to face death in a fierce struggle, but quite another to advance coldly upon it toward the muzzle of a pistol held so steadily that there could be no chance of escape. The gleam of determination in the man's eye convinced me he meant what he said. I did not consider then, nor have I considered since, that the next five minutes, precious as they were, would be worth paying my life for. Apparently everyone else was of my opinion, for none moved hand or foot until the clock slowly struck three.

"Thank you, gentlemen," said the American, as he vanished between the doors. When I say vanished, I mean that word and no other, because my men outside saw nothing of this individual then or later. He vanished as if he had never existed, and it was some hours before we found how this had been accomplished.

I rushed out almost on his heels, as one might say, and hurriedly questioned my waiting men. They had all seen the tall American come out with the greatest leisureliness and stroll toward the west. As he was not the man any of them were looking for, they paid no further attention to him, as, indeed, is the custom with our Parisian force. They have eyes for nothing but what they are sent to look for, and this trait has its drawbacks for their superiors.

I ran up the boulevard, my whole thought intent on the diamonds and their owner. I knew my subordinate in command of the men inside the hall would look after the scoundrel with the pistols. A short distance up I found the stupid fellow I had sent out, standing in a dazed manner at the corner of the Rue Michodiere, gazing alternately down that short street and toward the Place de l'Opera. The very fact that he was there furnished proof that he had failed.

"Where is the American?" I demanded.

"He went down this street, sir."

"Then why are you standing here like a fool?"

"I followed him this far, when a man came up the Rue Michodiere, and without a word the American handed him the jewel box, turning instantly down the street up which the other had come. The other jumped into a cab, and drove toward the Place de l'Opera."

"And what did you do? Stood here like a post, I suppose?"

"I didn't know what to do, sir. It all happened in a moment."

"Why didn't you follow the cab?"

"I didn't know which to follow, sir, and the cab was gone instantly while I watched the American."

"What was its number?"

"I don't know, sir."

"You clod! Why didn't you call one of our men, whoever was nearest and leave him to shadow the American while you followed the cab?"

"I did shout to the nearest man, sir, but he said you told him to stay there and watch the English lord, and even before he had spoken, both American and cabman were out of sight."

"Was the man to whom he gave the box an American also?"

"No, sir, he was French."

"How do you know?"

"By his appearance and the words he spoke."

"I thought you said he didn't speak?"

"He did not speak to the American, sir, but he said to the cabman, 'Drive to the Madeleine as quickly as you can.' "

"Describe the man."

"He was a head shorter than the American, wore a black beard and mustache rather neatly trimmed, and seemed to be a superior sort of artisan."

"You did not take the number of the cab. Should you know the cabman if you saw him again?"

"Yes, sir, I think so."

Taking this fellow with me I returned to the now nearly empty auction room and there gathered all my men about me. Each in his notebook took down particulars of the cabman and his passenger from the lips of my competent spy; next I dictated a full description of the two Americans, then scattered my men to the various railway stations of the lines leading out of Paris, with orders to make inquiries of the police on duty there, and to arrest one or more of the four persons described should they be so fortunate as to find any of them.

I now learned how the rogue with the pistols vanished so completely as he did. My subordinate in the auction room had speedily solved the mystery. To the left of the main entrance of the auction room was a door that gave private access to the rear of the premises. As the attendant in charge confessed when questioned, he had been bribed by the American earlier in the day to leave this side door open and to allow the man to escape by the goods entrance. Thus the ruffian did not appear on the boulevard at all, and so had not been observed by any of my men.

Taking my futile spy with me I returned to my own office and sent an order throughout the city that every cabman who had been in the Boulevard des Italiens between half past two and half past three that afternoon should report immediately to me. The examination of these men proved a very tedious business indeed, but whatever other countries may say of us, we French are patient, and if the haystack is searched long enough the needle will be found. I did not discover the needle I was looking for, but I came upon one quite as important, if not more so.

It was nearly ten o'clock at night when a cabman answered my oft-repeated questions in the affirmative.

"Did you take up a passenger a few minutes past three o'clock on the Boulevard des Italiens, near the Credit-Lyonnais? Had he a short black beard? Did he carry a small box in his hand and order you to drive to the Madeleine?"

The cabman seemed puzzled. "He wore a short black beard when he got out of the cab," he replied.

"What do you mean by that?"

"I drive a closed cab, sir. When he got in he was a smooth faced gentleman; when he got out he wore a short black beard."

"Was he a Frenchman?"

"No, sir; he was a foreigner, either English or American."

"Was he carrying a box?"

"No, sir; he held in his hand a small leather bag."

"Where did he tell you to drive?"

"He told me to follow the cab in front, which had just driven off very rapidly toward the Madeleine. In fact, I heard the man, such as you describe, order the other cabman to drive to the Madeleine. I had come alongside the curb when this man held up his hand for a cab, but the open cab cut in ahead of me. Just then my passenger stepped up and said in French, but with a foreign accent: 'Follow that cab wherever it goes.' "

I turned with some inclination to my inefficient spy. "You told me," I said, "that the American had gone down a side street. Yet he evidently met a second man, obtained from him the handbag, turned back, and into the closed cab directly behind you."

"Well, sir," stammered the spy, "I could not look in two directions at the same time. The American certainly went down the side street, but of course I watched the cab which contained the jewels."

"And you saw nothing of the closed cab right at your elbow?"

"The boulevard was full of cabs, sir, and the pavement crowded with passersby, as it always is at that hour of the day, and I have only two eyes in my head."

"I am glad to know you had that many, for I was beginning to think you were blind."

Although I said this, I knew in my heart it was useless to censure the poor wretch, for the fault was entirely my own in not sending two men, and in failing to guess the possibility of the jewels and their owner being separated. Besides, here was a clue to my hand at last, and no time must be lost in following it up. So I continued my interrogation of the cabman. "The other cab was an open vehicle, you say?"

"Yes, sir."

"You succeeded in following it?"

"Oh, yes, sir. At the Madeleine the man in front redirected the coachman, who turned to the left and drove to the Place de la Concorde, then up the Champs Elysees to the Arc and so down the Avenue de la Grande Armee, and the Avenue de Neuilly, to the Pont de Neuilly, where it came to a standstill. My fare got out, and I saw he now wore a short black beard, which he had evidently put on inside the cab. He gave me a ten-franc piece, which was very satisfactory."

"And the fare you were following? What did he do?"

"He also stepped out, paid the cabman, went down the bank of the river and got on board a steam launch that seemed to be waiting for him."

"Did he look behind, or appear to know that he was being followed?"

"No, sir."

"And your fare?"

"He ran after the first man, and also went aboard the steam launch, which instantly started down the river."

"And that was the last you saw of them?"

"Yes, sir."

"At what time did you reach the Pont de Neuilly?"

The Mystery of the Five Hundred Diamonds

"I do not know, sir; I was compelled to drive rather fast, but the distance is seven or eight kilometers."

"You would do it under the hour?"

"But certainly, under the hour."

"Then you must have reached Neuilly bridge about four o'clock?"

"It is very likely, sir."

The plan of the tall American was now perfectly clear to me, and it comprised nothing that was contrary to law. He had evidently placed his luggage on board the steam launch in the morning. The handbag had contained various materials which would enable him to disguise himself, and this bag he had probably left in some shop down the side street, or else some one was waiting with it for him. The giving of the treasure to another man was not so risky as it had at first appeared, because he instantly followed that man, who was probably his confidential servant. Despite the windings of the river there was ample time for the launch to reach Havre before the American steamer sailed on Saturday morning. I surmised it was his intention to come alongside the steamer before she left her berth in Havre harbor, and thus transfer himself and his belongings unperceived by anyone on watch at the land side of the liner.

All this, of course, was perfectly justifiable, and seemed, in truth, merely a well-laid scheme for escaping observation. His only danger of being tracked was when he got into the cab. Once away from the neighborhood of the Boulevard des Italiens he was reasonably sure to evade pursuit, and the five minutes which his friend with the pistols had won for him afforded just the time he needed to get so far as the Place Madeleine. After that everything was easy. Yet, if it had not been for those five minutes secured by coercion, I should not have found the slightest excuse for arresting him. But he was accessory after the act in that piece of illegality—in fact, it was absolutely certain that he had been accessory before the act, and guilty of conspiracy with the man who had presented firearms to the auctioneer's audience, and who had interfered with an officer in the discharge of his duty by threatening me and my men. So I was now legally in the right if I arrested every person on board that steam launch.

Chapter III. The Midnight Race Down the Seine

With a map of the river before me, I proceeded to make some calculations. It was now nearly ten o'clock at night. The launch had had six hours in which to travel at its utmost speed. It was doubtful if so small a vessel could make ten miles an hour, even with the current in its favor, which is rather sluggish because of the locks and the level country. Sixty miles would place her beyond Meulan, which is fifty-eight miles from the Pont Royal, and, of course, a lesser distance from the Pont de Kneel. But the navigation of the river is difficult at all times, and almost impossible after dark. There were chances of the boat running aground, and then there was the inevitable delay at the locks. So I estimated that the launch could not yet have reached Meulan, which was less than twenty-five miles from Paris by rail. Looking up the timetable I saw there were still two trains to Meulan, the next at 11:40. I therefore had time to reach St. Lazaret station, and accomplish some telegraphing before the train left.

With three of my assistants I got into a cab and drove to the station. On arrival I sent one of my men to hold the train while I went into the telegraph office, cleared the wires, and got into communication with the lock master at Meulan. He replied that no steam launch had passed down since an hour before sunset. I then instructed him to allow the yacht to enter the lock, close the upper gate, let half of the water out, and hold the vessel there until I came. I also ordered the local Meulan police to send enough men to the lock to enforce this command. Lastly, I sent messages all along the river asking the police to report to me on the train the passage of the steam launch.

The 10:25 is a slow train, stopping at every station. However, every drawback has its compensation, and these stoppages enabled me to receive and to send telegraphic messages. I was quite well aware that I might be on a fool's errand in going to Meulan. The yacht could have put about before it had steamed a mile, and so returned back to Paris. There had been no time to learn whether this was so or not if I was to catch the 10:25. Also, it might have landed its passengers anywhere along the river. I may say at once that neither of these two things happened, and my calculations regarding her movements were accurate to the letter. But a trap most carefully set may be prematurely sprung by inadvertence, or more often by the overzeal of some stupid fool who fails to understand his instructions, or oversteps them if they are understood.

I received a most annoying telegram from Denouval, a lock about thirteen miles above that of Meulan. The local policeman, arriving at the lock, found that the yacht had just cleared. The fool shouted to the captain to return, threatening him with all the pains and penalties of the law if he refused. The captain did refuse, rang on full speed ahead, and disappeared in the darkness. Through this well-meant blunder of an understrapper those on board the launch had received warning that we were on their track. I telegraphed to the lockkeeper at Denouval to allow no craft to pass toward Paris until further orders. We thus held the launch in a thirteen mile stretch of water, but the night was pitch dark, and passengers might be landed on either bank with all of France before them, over which to effect their escape in any direction.

It was midnight when I reached the lock at Meulan, and as was to be expected, nothing had been seen or heard of the launch. It gave me some satisfaction to telegraph to that dunderhead at Denouval to walk along the riverbank to Meulan, and report if he learned the launch's whereabouts. We took up our quarters in the lodgekeeper's house and waited. There was little use in sending men to scour the country at this time of night, for the pursued were on the alert, and very unlikely to allow themselves to be caught if they had gone ashore. On the other hand, there was every chance that the captain would refuse to let them land, because he must know his vessel was in a trap from which it could not escape. And although the demand of the policeman at Denouval was quite unauthorized, nevertheless the captain could not know that, while

he must be well aware of his danger in refusing to obey a command from the authorities. Even if he got away for the moment, he
must know that arrest was certain, and that his punishment would
be severe. His only plea could be that he had not heard and understood the order to return. But this plea would be invalidated if
he aided in the escape of two men, whom he must now know were
wanted by the police. I was therefore very confident that if his passengers asked to be set ashore, the captain would refuse when he
had had time to think about his own danger. My estimate proved
accurate, for toward one o'clock the lockkeeper came in and said
the green and red lights of an approaching craft were visible, and
as he spoke the yacht whistled for the opening of the lock. I stood
by the lockkeeper while he opened the gates; my men and the local
police were concealed on each side of the lock. The launch came
slowly in, and as soon as it had done so I asked the captain to step
ashore, which he did.

"I wish a word with you," I said. "Follow me."

I took him into the lockkeeper's house and closed the door.
"Where are you going?"

"To Havre."

"Where did you come from?"

"Paris."

"From what quay?"

"From the Pont de Kneel."

"When did you leave there?"

"At five minutes to four o'clock this afternoon."

"Yesterday afternoon, you mean?"

"Yesterday afternoon."

"Who engaged you to make this voyage?"

"An American; I do not know his name."

"He paid you well, I suppose?"

"He paid me what I asked."

"Have you received the money?"

"Yes, sir."

"I may inform you, captain, that I am Eugene Valmont, chief detective of the French government, and that all the police of France at this moment are under my control. I ask you, therefore, to be careful of your answers. You were ordered by a policeman at Denouval to return. Why did you not do so?"

"The lockkeeper ordered me to return, but as he had no right to order me, I went on."

"You know very well it was the police who ordered you, and you ignored the command. Again I ask you why you did so."

"I did not know it was the police."

"I thought you would say that. You knew very well, but were paid to take the risk, and it is likely to cost you dear. You had two passengers aboard?"

"Yes, sir."

"Did you put them ashore between here and Denouval?"

"No, sir; but one of them went overboard, and we couldn't find him again."

"Which one?"

"The short man."

"Then the American is still aboard?"

"What American, sir?"

"Captain, you must not trifle with me. The man who engaged you is still aboard?"

"Oh, no, sir, he has never been aboard."

"Do you mean to tell me that the second man who came on your launch at the Pont de Kneel is not the American who engaged you?"

"No, sir; the American was a smooth faced man; this man wore a black beard."

"Yes, a false beard."

"I did not know that, sir. I understood from the American that I was to take but one passenger. One came aboard with a small box in his hand; the other with a small bag. Each declared himself to be the passenger in question. I did not know what to do, so I left Paris with both of them on board."

"Then the tall man with the black beard is still with you?"

"Yes, sir."

"Well, captain, is there anything else you have to tell me? I think you will find it better in the end to make a clean breast of it."

The captain hesitated, turning his cap about in his hands for a few moments; then he said, "I am not sure that the first passenger went overboard of his own accord. When the police hailed us at Denouval—"

"Ah! you knew it was the police, then?"

"I was afraid after I left it might have been. You see, when the bargain was made with me the American said that if I reached Havre at a certain time, a thousand francs extra would be paid to me, so I was anxious to get along as quickly as I could. I told him it was dangerous to navigate the Seine at night, but he paid me well for attempting it. After the policeman called to us at Denouval, the man with the small box became very much excited, and asked me to put him ashore, which I refused to do. The tall man appeared to be watching him, never letting him get far away. When I heard the splash in the water I ran aft, and I saw the tall man putting the box which the other had held into his handbag, although I said nothing of it at the time. We cruised back and forth about the spot where the other man had gone overboard, but saw nothing more of him. Then I came on to Meulan, intending to give information about what I had seen. That is all I know of the matter, sir."

"Was the man who had the jewels a Frenchman?"

"What jewels, sir?"

"The man with the small box."

"Oh, yes, sir; he was French."

The Mystery of the Five Hundred Diamonds

"You have hinted that the foreigner threw him overboard. What grounds have you for such a belief if you did not see the struggle?"

"The night is very dark, sir, and I did not see what happened. I was at the wheel in the forward part of the launch, with my back turned to these two. I heard a scream, then a splash. If the man had jumped overboard as the other said he did, he would not have screamed. Besides, as I told you, when I ran aft I saw the foreigner put the little box in his handbag, which he shut up quickly as if he did not wish me to notice."

"Very good, captain. If you have told the truth it will go easy with you in the investigation that is to follow."

I now turned the captain over to one of my men, and ordered in the foreigner with his bag and bogus black whiskers. Before questioning him, I ordered him to open the handbag, which he did with evident reluctance. It was filled with false whiskers, false mustaches, and various bottles, but on top of them all lay the jewel case. I raised the lid and displayed that accursed necklace. I looked up at the man, who stood there calmly enough, saying nothing in spite of the overwhelming evidence against him.

"Will you oblige me by removing your false beard?"

"He did so at once, throwing it into the open bag. I knew the moment I saw him that he was not the American, and thus my theory had broken down, in one very important part at least. Informing him who I was, and cautioning him to speak the truth, I asked how he came in possession of the jewels.

"Am I under arrest?" he asked.

"But certainly," I replied.

"Of what am I accused?"

"You are accused, in the first place, of being in possession of property which does not belong to you."

"I plead guilty to that. What in the second place?"

"In the second place, you may find yourself accused of murder."

"I am innocent of the second charge. The man jumped overboard."

"If that is true, why did he scream as he went over?"

"Because, too late to recover his balance, I seized this box and held it."

"He was in rightful possession of the box; the owner gave it to him."

"I admit that; I saw the owner give it to him."

"Then why should he jump overboard?"

"I do not know. He seemed to become panic-stricken when the police at the last lock ordered us to return. He implored the captain to put him ashore, and from that moment I watched him keenly, expecting that if we drew near to the land he would attempt to escape, as the captain had refused to beach the launch. He remained quiet for about half an hour seated on a camp chair by the rail, with his eyes turned toward the shore, trying, as I imagined, to penetrate the darkness and estimate the distance. Then suddenly he sprang up and made his dash. I was prepared for this and instantly caught the box from his hand. He gave a half-turn, trying either to save himself or to retain the box; then with a scream went down shoulders first into the water. It all happened within a second after he leaped from his chair."

"You admit yourself, then, indirectly at least, responsible for his drowning?"

"I see no reason to suppose that the man was drowned. If able to swim, he could easily have reached the riverbank. If unable to swim, why should he attempt it encumbered by the box?"

"You believe he escaped then?"

"I think so."

"It will be lucky for you should that prove to be the case."

"Certainly."

"How did you come to be in the yacht at all?"

The Mystery of the Five Hundred Diamonds

"I shall give you a full account of the affair, concealing nothing. I am a private detective, with an office in London. I was certain that some attempt would be made, probably by the most expert criminals at large, to rob the possessor of this necklace. I came over to Paris, anticipating trouble, determined to keep an eye upon the jewel case if this proved possible. If the jewels were stolen, the crime was bound to be one of the most celebrated in legal annals. I was present during the sale, and saw the buyer of the necklace. I followed the official who went to the bank, and thus learned that the money was behind the check. I then stopped outside and waited for the buyer to appear. He held the case in his hand.

"In his pocket, you mean?" I interrupted.

"He had it in his hand when I saw him. Then the man who afterwards jumped overboard approached him, took the case without a word, held up his hand for a cab, and when an open vehicle approached the curb he stepped in, saying, 'The Madeleine.' I hailed a closed cab, instructed the cabman to follow the first, disguising myself with whiskers as near like those the man in front wore as I had in my collection."

"Why did you do that?"

"As a detective you should know why I did it. I wished as nearly as possible to resemble the man in front, so that if necessity arose I could pretend that I was the person commissioned to carry the jewel case. As a matter of fact, the crisis arose when we came to the end of our cab journey. The captain did not know which was his true passenger, and so let us both remain aboard the launch. And now you have the whole story."

"An extremely improbable one, sir. Even by your own account you had no right to interfere in this business at all."

"I quite agree with you there," he replied, with great nonchalance, taking a card from his pocketbook, which he handed to me.

"That is my London address; you may make inquiries, and you will find I am exactly what I represent myself to be."

The first train for Paris left Meulan at eleven minutes past four in the morning. It was now a quarter of two. I left the captain, crew, and launch in charge of two of my men, with orders to proceed to Paris as soon as it was daylight. I, supported by the third man, waited at the station with our English prisoner, and reached Paris at half past five in the morning.

The English prisoner, though severely interrogated by the judge, stood by his story. Inquiry by the police in London proved that what he said of himself was true. His case, however, began to look very serious when two of the men from the launch asserted that they had seen him push the Frenchman overboard, and their statements could not be shaken. All our energies were bent for the next two weeks on trying to find something of the identity of the missing man, or to get any trace of the two Americans. If the tall American were alive, it seemed incredible that he should not have made application for the valuable property he had lost. All attempts to trace him by means of the check on the Credit-Lyonnais proved futile. The bank pretended to give me every assistance, but I sometimes doubt if it actually did so. It had evidently been well paid for its services, and demonstrated no great desire to betray so good a customer.

We made inquiries about every missing man in Paris, but also without result.

The case had excited much attention throughout the world, and doubtless was published in full in the American papers. The Englishman had been in custody three weeks when the Chief of Police in Paris received the following letter:

Dear Sir:

> On my arrival in New York by the English steamer *Lucania,* I was much amused to read in the papers accounts of the exploits of detectives, French and English. I am sorry that only one of them seems to be in prison; I think his French colleague ought to be there also. I regret exceedingly, however, that there is rumor of the death by drowning of my friend Martin Dubois, of 375 Rue aux Juifs, Rouen. If this is indeed the case, he has met his death through the blunders of the police. Nevertheless, I wish you would communicate

with his family at the address I have given, and assure them that I will make arrangements for their future support.

I beg to inform you that I am a manufacturer of imitation diamonds, and through extensive advertising succeeded in accumulating a fortune of many millions. I was in Europe when the necklace was found, and had in my possession over a thousand imitation diamonds of my own manufacture. It occurred to me that here was the opportunity of the most magnificent advertisement in the world. I saw the necklace, received its measurements, and also obtained photographs of it taken by the French government. Then I set my expert friend Martin Dubois at work, and with the artificial stones I gave him he made an imitation necklace so closely resembling the original that you apparently do not know it is the unreal you have in your possession. I did not fear the villainy of the crooks as much as the blundering of the police, who would have protected me with brass band vehemence if I could not elude them.

I knew that the detectives would overlook the obvious, but would at once follow a clue if I provided one for them. Consequently, I laid my plans, just as you have discovered, and got Martin Dubois up from Rouen to carry the case I gave him down to Havre. I had had another box prepared and wrapped in brown paper, with my address in New York written thereon. The moment I emerged from the auction room, while my friend the cowboy was holding up the audience, I turned my face to the door, took out the genuine diamonds from the case and slipped it into the box I had prepared for mailing. Into the genuine case I put the bogus diamonds. After handing the box to Dubois, I turned down a side street, and then into another whose name I do not know, and there in a shop with sealing wax and string did up the real diamonds for posting. I labeled the package "Books," went to the nearest post office, paid letter postage, and handed it over unregistered, as if it were of no particular value.

After this I went to my rooms in the Grand Hotel, where I had been staying under my own name for more than a month. Next morning I took the train for London, and the day after sailed from Liverpool on the Lucania. I arrived before the Gascogne, which sailed to Havre on Saturday, met my box at the customhouse, paid duty, and it now reposes in my safe.

I intend to construct an imitation necklace which will be so like the genuine one that nobody can tell the two apart; then I shall come to Europe and exhibit the pair, for the publication of the truth of this matter will give me the greatest advertisement that ever was.

Yours truly, John P. Hazard

I at once communicated with Rouen and found Martin Dubois alive and well. His first words were: "I swear I did not steal the jewels."

He had swum ashore, tramped to Rouen, and kept quiet in great fear while I was fruitlessly searching Paris for him.

It took Mr. Hazard longer to make his imitation necklace than he supposed, and several years later he booked his passage with the two necklaces on the ill-fated steamer *Bourgogne*, and now rests beside them at the bottom of the Atlantic.

As the English poet says:
Full many a gem of purest ray serene,
The dark unfathomed caves of ocean bear.

About the Author

Robert Barr (1850-1912) was born in Glasgow, Scotland. He was both an editor and an author.

"The Mystery of the Five Hundred Diamonds" first appeared in the Windsor Magazine *in 1904. Two years later the story was published in the book* The Triumphs of Eugene Valmont.